The
MALDONADO
Miracle

THEODORE TAYLOR

The MALDONADO Miracle

Harcourt, Inc.

ORLANDO   AUSTIN   NEW YORK
SAN DIEGO   TORONTO   LONDON

www.HarcourtBooks.com

Portions of this novel have appeared in *Redbook* magazine
under the title "A Test of Faith,"
copyright © 1962 by McCall Corporation.

First published by Doubleday & Company, Inc. in 1973
First paperback edition published by Avon Books, Inc. in 1986

Library of Congress Cataloging-in-Publication Data
Taylor, Theodore, 1921–
The Maldonado miracle/Theodore Taylor.
p. cm.
Reprint. Originally published: New York: Doubleday, 1973;
first pbk. ed.: New York: Avon Books, 1986.
Summary: A twelve-year-old Mexican crosses
the border illegally to join his father in California.
[1. Illegal aliens—Fiction. 2. Mexicans—United States—Fiction.
3. Migrant labor—Fiction.] I. Title.
PZ7.T2186Mal   2003
[Fic]—dc21   2003045283
ISBN 0-15-205037-X
ISBN 0-15-205036-1 (pb)

Text set in Dante
Designed by Lydia D'moch

A C E G H F D B
C E G H F D (pb)

Printed in the United States of America

To Gwen, with Love

Book I

THE NEW LIFE

1

GUTIERREZ WAS pointing to a much-used Pemex road map spread over an up-ended wooden crate. He said, "Now, pay attention. You will cross here late tonight. I will already have gone through customs and immigration. Look closely. Right here."

The heavy finger was at a place in California opposite the Mexican border town of Tecate.

Jose glanced over at the stranger from San Diego. He was a stocky man about forty. A *pocho,* an American of Mexican descent. He was speaking in Spanish because Jose understood very little English.

Jose nodded, but his legs suddenly felt weak. It was the same old problem. He knew he should be excited, but all he felt was fear.

Gutierrez went on as if he did this several times a week. "You'll ride in the trunk of my car until we are far away from the border. Many people make the mistake of traveling the big highway, and they are caught here at the checkpoint near Oceanside." The thick finger tapped again.

Jose thought about men in uniform holding a flashlight to his face; a ride to jail in a patrol car.

"We won't do that," Gutierrez said. "We'll go on the back roads. East to Jacumba, then north again up through Pine Valley, here by Escondido, taking a dirt road to skirt another roadblock, then on to Elsinore, and finally back on the main road here at San Juan Capistrano."

With the exception of that last place, where there was a famous mission, Jose had never heard of any of them. He studied the map and tried to make his voice deeper, more manly. "Is this the best way?"

Gutierrez nodded and removed his glasses, tucking them into his shirt pocket. He smelled of hair tonic. "Yes, Jose. Your father agreed. We'll pick him up in Oxnard tomorrow. All the arrangements have been made."

Jose wondered what the arrangements were; where Oxnard was. He wished he'd been able to talk to his father, though not much would have resulted.

"Except that you are skinny, you don't look like your father. You don't have his height," Gutierrez commented.

That was true.

Over six feet tall, Hector Maldonado Alvarez had very little meat on him. When he had his shirt off and was lifting something heavy, his ribs projected like steel rims. His face was sharp and bony, like his wrists. It was a mellow red-brown. He had told Jose that their blood was Spanish and Indian.

Jose was short, wiry, black-haired. His large, soft eyes were unlike those of his father. They were his mother's eyes. Long lashed.

Slightly embarrassed, and not knowing what else to say, Jose answered simply, "No, I do not." He reached down to scrub Sanchez's thick neck.

The big mongrel had been watching Gutierrez from the moment the old car had driven up. He was splotched black and brown and had one discolored eye. It was greenish. His coat was like a matted, worn shag rug. His head seemed oversized for his body, the nose flat like a cow's. His tail had been accidentally mashed off midway, so that it was neither long nor short. It looked strange, especially because hair refused to grow on the last inch of it. There was nothing there but gray skin.

Gutierrez shifted on his sandals. "The money," he said. "Half now."

For a moment, Jose thought about what to do. Then he said, "Go outside, please, *señor*."

Gutierrez laughed. "I am doing your father a favor. Don't be suspicious of me, boy." But he shrugged and waddled out into the sunlight.

Jose dragged the empty box to the rear of the room and stood up on it, feeling along the top of the beam beneath the tile roof for the stack of bills. He had counted them a dozen times. The other half of the smuggling fee, payable after Gutierrez delivered Jose to his father and then took them on somewhere else, was buried outside in a coffee can.

Dropping down off the box, he counted it once again and then joined Gutierrez in the yard.

The *pocho* was smiling, and Jose felt silly. After all, the money was for Gutierrez; his father had placed confidence in him. "Seventy-five dollars, American. Count it."

Gutierrez chuckled. "I don't need to. I'm sure you've done it fifty times."

Jose finally laughed. "A dozen, at least."

"How old are you?" Gutierrez asked, cramming the bills into his wallet.

"Twelve." He'd rather have been eight or six or five again.

Gutierrez nodded. "You've been here alone? How long?"

"Four months."

"Any trouble?"

Jose shook his head unconcernedly. "I have Sanchez. I've been quite safe. I haven't even thought about it." That was a lie. He'd spent many nights on the straw matting, his throat tight, listening to every sound. Finally falling asleep, one hand dug into Sanchez's fur.

Gutierrez smiled, glancing at the mammoth dog. Then his face became serious. "Don't panic tonight. Maldonado said to tell you to keep your guts. Immigration would lock me up and throw away the key if they caught me with a child."

Momentarily resenting being called a child, Jose said, "I will try not to panic." There was that word again. Try. His stomach ticked at the thoughts of immigration, *la migra*.

"Good." Gutierrez turned and went over to the dusty Chevrolet. The starter ground as if it had a bellyache; then the engine caught and revved. "This time tomorrow, we'll be far past Los Angeles," he called out cheerfully.

Keep his guts! It sounded so easy.

Gutierrez waved and headed back up the bumpy dirt road toward Baja No. 1, the rolling blacktop that stretched from Tijuana south to Colonia Guerrero, a few miles below Cabo Colnett, the great blunt-headed cape. The pavement ended there. Beyond that there was little but wilderness all the way to Cabo San Lucas, at the tip of the peninsula.

Jose watched the car with U.S. plates bounce and rock around the bend, disappearing in a rattling plume of dust. He stood a moment longer and let the quietness of the land descend on him. Finally, shivering involuntarily, he went back into the house.

The neat adobe showed only traces of people having once lived in it. A calendar. Hooks where his mother had hung pots. Several oblongs where she'd hung photographs of her family. Pegs that once held clothes. Smoke stains on beams from lanterns. Lifetime scars of three people.

Jose had sold off practically everything to get the money for Gutierrez: the chickens, the goat, the cow, a pig, the old horse, several hand plows and some tools; the heavy rowboat, and a few pieces of furniture. It had been a responsibility that had caused him to vomit one morning. Was he getting enough for them? Would his father be pleased?

Their friend Enrique had borrowed a pickup and they'd taken the few things Maldonado said he wanted to keep, mostly things that had belonged to Jose's mother, over to the cousin at Camalu down the road. Someday, Jose hoped, they'd return for them.

Now, with all the animals except Sanchez gone, the place seemed abandoned already. There had often been laughter here, especially while his mother was alive, and smells of pork and beef and chicken and fish cooked with lime and salt. Only Sunday past, neighbors and relatives had brought food and tequila and beer to wish him safety and good luck. Everyone was in good spirits. Some of the men got drunk; the women talked; the children played. Jose had felt very important, though he knew it was really a tribute to his father.

Maldonado was much admired around Colnett. If there was trouble out by the cape, everyone ran for Maldonado. Truck stuck in the winter mud; cow sick; two neighbors feuding; outboard motor busted. Call for Maldonado. They missed him, Jose knew.

———

THE LAST NINE MONTHS had been hard ones. In January, Jose's mother had died in Del Carmen hospital in Ensenada. She'd been ill with cancer for a long time. The doctor said there was no cure.

They'd buried her up by Baja 1 with Maldonado standing stiffly, straw hat in his horny hands, not weeping. Saying nothing. Dark eyes a thousand kilometers away in some endless cave.

Jose was glad that neighbors and relatives had been there because they had talked about her while Maldonado went for a long walk.

After that their luck had continued bad. In March, the land on which the Maldonados lived and cropped, with a share going to the Tijuana businessman who owned it, was sold to Mexico City developers. Soon, a representative from the company had visited the adobe.

"*Señor* Maldonado, you must understand. I beg you to understand. Simply, we have never been in the business of tenant farming. We do not intend to start now. I'm certain you can find other land..."

Maldonado kept staring.

"We are developers, Maldonado. I'm surprised the owner did not notify you when we bought these acres."

The young man looked around uncomfortably. "This will be a deluxe mobile home estate like the one at Estero. For American tourists. You know the place at Estero?"

Maldonado did not answer. Not even nod.

"Jobs will be created here. Now, if you know anything about construction, why . . ."

"I am a farmer. How long do we have?"

"Oh, some months."

"How long?"

"September."

Jose's father had looked at the expensively dressed young man from the *Distrito Federal* and had slowly shaken his head. Then he'd said, so quietly it seemed dangerous, "Get out."

But it was more his mother's death, Jose thought, than the Mexico City company, that had caused his father to cross the border for work.

The adobe was filled with memories.

2

"HE CAME AT NOON," Jose told Fernando Garcia, who lived out by the blacktop and was also twelve. Fernando had a round face, like a brown pumpkin, and deep dimples.

"Your father finally sent him? I did not think he would ever come."

"Neither did I."

"How will he do it?"

"In the trunk of his car."

"And you aren't afraid?"

Jose shook his head. He was glad Fernando could not see the sweat in the palm of his hands or look through his pant legs at his knees.

"You will not believe it up there, I promise," Fernando said. He'd been to the *Estados Unidos* twice with his parents. They ran the store at Colnett.

"I'm very excited, Fernando. I am."

"You don't act like it. Did your father have a message?"

"Oh, yes."

"What did he say?"

"He said he was fine and was waiting for me at a place called Oxnard. He already has a job as a foreman."

"He's a wetback, Jose," Fernando said. "You know that's not true."

"It is true, Fernando. He's a foreman. He's been up there four months. You know how good my father is at everything he does."

Fernando shrugged and sent the swing rope high into the air. The rubber tire was a looping black doughnut.

They were out by the great oak, in the sun-filtered dell that banked the dried creek bed, across the road from the Garcia house. The same road wound on down to the sea, passing the Maldonados' at one point. They'd played here for years.

"What will you do?"

"Fernando, I've told you. I'll go to school, like everyone else."

Fernando sighed. "And I've told you that wetbacks cannot go to school up there. I know."

"My father will arrange it."

"Jose, it is not a field that he can plant or a motor he can fix. There are authorities up there. You will be like a criminal."

Jose wished that he had not come up the road. He had

come to say good-bye, not to hear these words or argue with Fernando.

Though there was doubt in his eyes, Fernando finally smiled. "Yes." They had been friends for a long time. "Write me, will you?"

"When I can. *Adios.*"

They shook hands, and Jose called for Sanchez, who was rooting around in the creek bed, looking for lizards that sought the scant moisture beneath the rocks.

The boy and dog went west along the road.

WHY WAS IT he could not tell Fernando that he was so frightened his stomach had turned into dough? And why did he have to lie about Maldonado being a foreman? And about Maldonado sending word that he was fine? Keep your guts! Well, he didn't want to admit that message.

He walked along, scuffing the dust.

There were many things about his father he did not understand. Sometimes it seemed that Maldonado thought he was twenty years old. That he had always been twenty.

"Jose, can't you lift that?"

"Papa, I'm trying."

"The bolt goes this way, Jose. Not that way. Use your eyes. You're not a child."

"Yes, Papa."

"You tell the horse what to do. The horse doesn't tell you."

"Yes, Papa."

"You have all the confidence of a rabbit, Jose."

A rabbit. A sheep. A goat. Confidence. It was hard to get, especially around Colnett.

Maldonado had so much of it. He did not seem to be afraid of anything. No man. No animal. Not even the dangerous creatures. Jose had seen him flick a poised scorpion with his fingernail. Another time, when he didn't have his hoe, he'd stomped a snake's head with his boot heel. And he did it without even thinking about it.

Yet there was one thing. The church. The Virgin Mary. God. Even priests. Maldonado prayed every morning. In the fields, he'd sometimes stop and look up to heaven.

"Papa, look at my drawings."

"They're okay. Tomorrow we plant beans."

"Hector, look at his drawings. They're beautiful. He has talent. You should be proud."

"I am. I'll look at them tonight. Jose, how much did the cow give this morning?"

"Three litres."

"You still haven't learned how to do it."

"I'm trying, Papa."

He could hear his mother's voice. "They are beautiful drawings, Jose." Then a whisper. "I will try to get you some regular paper so you won't have to draw on bags."

When she was around, it was different. Maldonado was still Maldonado. But she was a bridge. Sometimes a fort.

"I'll teach you to be the best farmer in Baja."

"I don't think he wants to be a farmer, Hector."

"What do you want to be, Jose?"

"I don't know." He was afraid to say.

"He wants to be an artist. Like Orozco."

"I've never heard of him."

Maldonado had not had an easy life as a boy, Jose knew. He had never really been a boy. Perhaps that was why he didn't understand.

"I was behind a plow when I was five, Jose. It didn't hurt me."

"But, Hector, isn't it lucky that Jose can go to school?"

"I suppose."

THE DRAWINGS.

"I did this of you, Papa."

"Well, I guess it looks like me. But my ears aren't that big."

"I will do another one and make the ears smaller."

Another one and another one and another one. He could draw his mother easily—the large eyes and high cheekbones, the full lips, shining hair pulled back. But he always had difficulty with his father.

3

AT THE ADOBE, Jose sat on the low rock wall for a while, looking around, then got up to go inside and open his fiber suitcase again. There was nothing more to pack. Everything he owned was in it. Breeze poured through the open windows into the two bare rooms.

He returned to the wall and sat down again. He was glad he would not be there when the bulldozer bit into the weathered clay. One crunching sweep and the house would be a pile of rubble.

The laundry line was still up, stretched between a tree and a post. Once, he had done a drawing of his mother hanging shirts. It had not seemed important to keep it then. Now, he wished he had it.

"Someday you'll be in a museum, in a gold frame behind a velvet rope."

She'd laughed. "Jose, you're such a dreamer. No wonder your father gets upset with you."

It was a bad habit, he knew. That dreaming. But often, after all the work was finished, there wasn't much to do except dream. Go up to Fernando's or out to the ocean to see Enrique or make the long walk into Colnett village or the even longer one to the Camalu cousin.

Yet it had not been bad, especially during the school months, and there was always the future to think about. Perhaps a job in Tijuana or Mexicali. Once, he'd seen a man in Ensenada finishing furniture. He was rubbing wax on it, making the grain deep and glistening. Perhaps a man like that would need an apprentice.

"Don't set your goal on Tijuana, Jose. Think of Ciudad de Méjico."

The mere thought of Mexico City took his breath away. It was across the world. "Have you ever been there?"

"No," his mother said. "You know I haven't. But I know people who have. It is a great city. Millions of people."

It was hard to believe that there were a million people anywhere. "What would I do?"

"Go to art school. Use the talent God gave you."

Somehow she'd found the money to buy him an expensive book on the life of Orozco, the famous Mexican painter. He'd read it over and over again, keeping it wrapped in heavy paper.

So the dreams would go on.

HE KEPT looking around.

The well.

It had awakened him on countless dawns. The whirring of the spool, the faint splash, and then the creak as his mother had drawn up the first full bucket of the day. She had told him, when he was very small, an incredible thing—there were towns in the *Estados Unidos* where every house had running water. She'd never traveled farther north than Tijuana or Mexicali, but she knew many things.

The outdoor oven.

Its blackened mouth, set in the mound of clay that was like a high turtle's back, had breathed out overpowering smells while she was still alive. He could see her waving the smoke away from her face, bending down, careful not to step on spilled embers with her bare feet. No matter what, they'd always eaten well. And he'd never lacked for clothes or shoes.

The animal shelter.

It was hardly a barn. Just some tin on posts with board sides to keep the horse and cow out of the rain and provide a place for the hens to nest. Beyond that, the barbed wire enclosure for the pigs. They roamed anyway, squealing and scattering when a truck slugged down the road. He'd drawn that, too, but it hadn't seemed important to keep it.

He looked at the flower bed that was to the left of the adobe, shielded from the almost constant wind. Most of them were dried up now. Only the tough geraniums still lived. He hadn't watered it in more than a month. His mother had always taken good care of it, cutting flowers to brighten up inside. She'd said it hurt her when they withered away.

One of the last things she'd said to him was "Don't get old before your time, Jose."

Yet he had the feeling this afternoon that his boyhood was over, even though he was not prepared for more. That was another thing he did not wish to dwell on.

He took a final look, fixing the place in his mind, thinking that someday he might try to draw it as it appeared now, with the wind rippling the trees and the dust already beginning to collect on the doorstep.

He jumped down off the wall.

4

JOSE HAD ONE FINAL CHORE—take Sanchez to Enrique's for safekeeping and say good-bye to the fisherman, though they'd done that a good five times on Sunday.

Enrique's place was two kilometers on down the sandy road which jogged in and out past Maldonado's small field of corn, splitting into two roads where a winter wash cut it. Cars or trucks going to Meling Fishing Camp, and sometimes *americano* campers or jeeps, bucked and ground over its ruts. But there weren't more than twenty vehicles of any kind each day, even in summer. Jose often thought it was the loneliest place on earth.

Enrique's shack stood at the point where the Maldonados' road converged on the trail that led north and south along the beach bluff. He'd simply come and erected the driftwood and tin shack on the low cliff over the ocean without asking anyone. He'd been squatting there for years, fishing and digging clams; taking abalone off the rocks at low tide or trapping *langosta,* the clawless lobsters.

Trudging along the road, crisscrossed here and there with the light tracks of rattlesnakes on the fine sand, Sanchez padding by his knees, Jose thought of the conversation he'd had with his father that night in April when Maldonado had decided to go to California.

"Isn't it illegal?" Jose had asked.

Maldonado's eyes had been grave. "Yes, but the other way it might take years. So many papers. A lawyer. I cannot wait. There is nothing here for me to do."

"Suppose you are caught?"

"They will simply send me back. I know other men who have been sent back. It is no lasting disgrace." He had been up there and knew about such things.

A long time before, after two severe droughts on the west coast of Baja, Maldonado had worked as a *bracero,* a contract field laborer, in the United States. For several summers he would leave Colnett and go to Mexicali in late spring. There was a government employment center there, and the men would cross to El Centro, California, in a bus. They would be gone for a few months and then return, the bus roof stacked high with rope-tied cartons which had once held lettuce or celery but now held clothes and gifts.

Jose had met the bus with his mother, driving up with relatives. It was a happy occasion, and they'd had a fine meal in a Mexicali cafe each time.

"If everything is all right, I'll send for you," Maldonado had said.

"And I will have to cross the border without papers?"

His father had been reluctant to answer but finally said, "It is nothing."

Nothing?

There'd been so many questions Jose had wanted to ask. About where they'd live, and what they'd do; about school. He'd been going to the three-room school near Colnett, just to the north. But his father had waved all the questions aside. Instead, he'd talked about the wonderful things he'd seen in California: the huge highways, the great buildings and stores, the fine homes. Once, coming in a bus from the San Joaquin Valley he had seen the lights of Los Angeles from the top of a mountain range. They were without end, he said.

He'd never been so talkative. He'd talked on about having running water, an indoor toilet, electricity, a TV set, a motorbike; maybe even a car. Jose couldn't sleep after Maldonado had turned off their white gas lantern.

LICK, THE MANGY yellow hound that guarded Enrique's while he was out on the boat or clam digging, began making a fuss as they approached but quieted down when he recognized them. He growled at Sanchez and stiffened his back hairs, but they had long ago fought it out. Now, they'd have to learn to live with each other.

Jose went on around the shack and looked out across

the kelp beds. He spotted Enrique about a mile offshore. Usually, there were big sugar bass under the tangled beds.

He "hallo-ed" across the smooth, glistening sea until Enrique finally turned and waved. The words "A few more minutes" carried back faintly on the light wind.

Jose went over and sat down by the shack, Sanchez following him to slump by his feet. He looked over to the northwest. Great Colnett always seemed to be sleeping, even when the sun glared down on it. When the weather was foggy or hazy, it was like a huge gray bear in hibernation. From its high brow, there was nothing to be seen along the shore until the Meling camp; then really nothing more for thirty or forty kilometers below. At night, in clear weather, you could not see more than three lights— gas lanterns—for thirty kilometers in either direction.

There was just kelp-littered beach, with round polished rocks grinding in the wash of the surf up near the low cliff shoulders. Thousands of gulls and the constant wide vees of flapping pelicans.

Jose listened to the clink and swish as the waves tumbled the rocks against each other. For a moment, he watched the gulls, staying in the wind and then wheeling down to make a noisy pass at the water for sardines. He studied the undulating wings of the pelicans. On shore, they were funny, awkward birds, but in the Colnett sky, they seemed dignified and graceful.

Then he heard the backfire of an outboard and a steady hum. Enrique was skimming toward shore.

He turned back in the direction of their house. His father had been wise to choose it. In the harsh land around them there was a narrow strip of sweet-water earth, cupped down between low hills, cactus-dotted and home to rattlesnakes and coyote. This strip of land, set by a small willow grove, was like an oasis. His father had found the abandoned adobe and made a deal to crop the land before Jose was born.

To the northeast, the Sierra de Juárez towered. Directly opposite Colnett was a smaller range, the Sierra San Pedro Mártir. To the south and east, above San Quintín, was the snow-topped Cerro de la Encantada range—the enchanted mountains. His mother had once said, "This is the good land of the sleeping giants. You must paint it someday."

Jose noticed again how very beautiful it all was. Harsh, rugged and silent, but very beautiful.

He reached down, dug his fingers into Sanchez's coarse hairs and said softly, "I want to go very badly, but I will miss this and you."

He rose when he heard Enrique kill the outboard and went down to the beach.

In silence Enrique and Jose climbed the short but steep, loose-dirt bank. Jose always marveled that Enrique could climb it so easily with the outboard motor on his back. His legs were powerful, the calves bulging with muscle. His shoulders were wide.

As he was lowering the oily old two-cylinder engine

to the steps, Enrique said, "If I didn't hate cities so much, I'd go with you. But I would not last up there a week. My nose would rot or I would get into mischief." He laughed, taking the sopping burlap bag of gutted fish from Jose.

"I wish you were coming along," Jose said.

Enrique held up a hand in protest. "I'll get a beer, Jose, and we'll talk. All day, I've tried to think of things to have you tell Maldonado, but there's nothing to tell him except that the fishing is good, the clams are fat, and the game warden is still stupid."

Enrique stalked into the dark hut, which smelled of sweat and gas and fried fish.

"Gutierrez came," Jose said.

"Ah," Enrique said disgustedly, tossing the bag into a corner. "All those men are thieves. The ones who make the arrangements are called 'coyotes.' That's true. Gutierrez will be your coyote. He is also called a 'mule' because he is a driver, too. Down here, we call them 'chicken men.'"

A *pollero*, Jose thought. But he said, "He is a nice man."

"You hope." Enrique reached over to his battered table for a beer. "But I suppose Maldonado has talked to him. You tell him for me that if anything goes wrong, I'll cut his ears off."

Jose laughed, thinking it was good to have a friend like Enrique.

The fisherman popped the cap on the table edge, took a foaming drink of the warm beer and strode out the door. "I mean it," he said.

Outside, they stood in the coolness on the south side of the shack, shielded from the wind. Enrique asked, "Is there anything else I can do?"

Jose shook his head. "Just take good care of Sanchez, as you promised." He looked over at the drowsing dog. His father had said Sanchez was probably the ugliest dog on earth. He was surely the smelliest. He was a mixture of twenty breeds.

"I'll do that," said Enrique seriously. "But he better learn to like fish more than he does now. Else he'll get skinny here."

Enrique's face was weathered from the blinding summer's sun and the winter winds that managed to dodge around Colnett. Jose had noticed that he seldom frowned. The wrinkles were put there by salt and sun. Keeping his eyes on the dog, Enrique said, "I won't even look when I go past the adobe now."

Jose knew he couldn't stay here much longer. It was too difficult. He stuck his hand out, but Enrique enclosed him in a fish-scaled bear hug and pounded his back.

"Go away," he said gruffly.

Jose went over to Sanchez. The dog came erect, eyes tense. He'd been nervous the past two weeks while the adobe was stripped and the animals sold off.

"You stay with Enrique and Lick until I come back, Sanchez. All right?"

The dog whimpered.

"Stay," Jose said.

Enrique, his head down, stepped over to grab the dog's scruff.

"Stay, I said," Jose repeated.

"You go on, Jose," Enrique snapped.

Jose whirled around and began walking up the road toward the adobe, setting his teeth tight now, swearing he would not look back. He heard low moans behind him; then a curse.

Jose stopped, knowing what had happened. Enrique was sprawled in the sand, beer splattered over his shirt.

Sanchez was three feet away, barking, demanding to go.

"Take that insane dog with you," Enrique shouted.

"I can't. My father would rage."

"Let him rage," Enrique shouted, and then Jose could hear him laughing.

"Gutierrez would not take him. Don't you see?"

"Tell Gutierrez not to act like an old lady. Tell Gutierrez I'll turn him in to the authorities unless he takes Sanchez—after I punch him in the mouth."

Jose grabbed Sanchez by the loose skin, and began walking back toward the hut, tugging the balking dog.

5

Jose was sitting in the front seat with Gutierrez, not saying much. As they turned onto Baja No. 1, across from the cemetery on the hillside where his mother was buried, near Bradey's, he crossed himself, acknowledging her, and then looked into the back seat, where Sanchez was perched triumphantly.

Gutierrez was still a little angry. He said, "I think that man Enrique is crazy. I don't like people threatening me."

Jose tried to keep from smiling. "He is not crazy."

A few minutes later, Gutierrez said, "Well, maybe it is best. If anyone sees you with a dog around the border they'll think you live in Tecate."

Jose nodded. He had been worrying about what his father might say when he saw Sanchez. It was like a thousand wild boar attacking, sudden as hail, when his father got angry.

The car moved past San Vicente and the narrow, lazy

San Ysidro River, on toward Santo Tomás and Maneadero. It was less than two hours to Ensenada, and the road was very good.

Jose looked out the window as the barren countryside swept by, wondering when he would see it again. It was almost six o'clock, and the sun was dull gold against the Juárez peaks. Beyond them, the sky was already darkening.

As near as he could remember, he had been to Ensenada six times, four of them just this winter when his mother was in the hospital. It had always seemed a large place. In comparison to the gas station, store, and cafe at San Vicente, it was as big as Mexico City.

He'd seen television for the first time in Ensenada when he was ten. Maldonado had gone there on business, taking Jose with him. A TV set had been in the window of a Calle Primera furniture store, and they had stood outside for more than two hours that Saturday morning to watch cartoons. Jose had wondered how it worked. Then this winter, he'd watched again, thinking that some day it might come to Colnett. Ensenada was a remarkable place.

As they passed the airport the traffic became heavy. He saw the new fried chicken shop, with the picture of the white-bearded *americano* on the big metal barrel. They'd stopped there after his mother died, to buy some chicken to eat while waiting for the bus south. He'd always remember that barrel turning round and round, just after they'd come from the hospital.

He looked over at Gutierrez. "*Señor*, I want to stop at the church before we go on to Tecate."

The *pocho* frowned.

"I'll only stay a moment."

"You believe in God?" Gutierrez asked.

"Yes, and the Virgin Mary. They are good to us, my father said. They look over us."

Gutierrez cleared his throat noisily but took the lane to Avenida Benito Juárez.

That day last winter they had gone to the church before walking on to the fried chicken shop. It was on a side street, by the market, several blocks past the traffic circle and the General Juárez monument.

Gutierrez waited in the car as Jose went in. He removed his hat, lit a candle, and prayed. He prayed for his mother, his father, himself, Sanchez, Enrique, and even Gutierrez. The routine was familiar. The Maldonados seldom missed Sunday mass in the small church near San Vicente. They always walked the blacktop and then caught a ride with the Camalu cousin.

As he was getting back into the car, Jose told Gutierrez, "I said a prayer for you. You, too, Sanchez."

The *pocho* cleared his throat again and backed out. Benito Juárez was jammed, and all the lights were on. Music came from loudspeakers at the stores that sold records. All the pushcart vendors were out, and the men who sold leather goods and *serapes* and silver jewelry from Taxco approached strolling *turistas*.

Gutierrez turned at Gastelum, and they left the city, picking up speed as they got to the freeway north. He turned once more at El Sauzal, by the ocean, a place Jose had never seen. Then they were on the road to Tecate. The Chevy hummed.

It was dark now, and Gutierrez began to talk. He took a drawing out of his shirt pocket.

Jose unfolded it and held it beneath the pale yellow light of the dash.

"There is a hole under the fence where I have put the red mark. It is covered with reeds. From the road, the fence looks solid. Just push the reeds aside and go under the fence."

"Is there water?" Jose asked.

"No water except when it rains, and that's not likely tonight. It's a drain. That's why the reeds are there. I'm surprised the border patrol hasn't found it."

Jose's heart began to thud in his ears.

"Just wait on the opposite side of the road until you are certain no cars are approaching. Then cross it quickly and keep low."

Jose nodded.

"You understand?"

"Yes, *señor*."

"I'll let you out in Hidalgo Park in Tecate. Then I'll drive on up and clear immigration and customs. You go to the border. I'll take your suitcase as if it was mine. I brought a few things of mine to put on top of yours."

Jose's suitcase was in the trunk of the car.

"Any questions?"

"No, *señor*." Jose turned and looked at Sanchez. The dog was asleep.

The way was mostly downhill now, over Baja No. 3, past open land and small, dimly lit villages. It was farm country, and the only large town was Guadalupe. Once they passed it, Jose knew that Tecate wasn't too far ahead. A half-hour at most.

After a long silence, he said suddenly, "Suppose the patrol finds me at the fence."

Gutierrez laughed. "You put your hands up, and be very polite. Very meek."

When the car stopped by the edge of Hidalgo Park, almost in the middle of Tecate, Jose whispered, "Sanchez, wake up." The dog rose to his feet.

As they got out, Gutierrez warned, "Act very natural, Jose. I'll see you in about forty-five minutes."

The door closed again, and Gutierrez muttered, "Good luck," and drove off up Lázaro Cardenas toward the border. Jose watched his taillights until they had vanished in the sparse traffic. It was about ten o'clock.

Jose stood under a streetlight for a moment, studying the route Gutierrez had drawn on brown paper. Finally, he folded it and stuck it into his pocket. Then he said, "We'll go now, Sanchez. Stay very close to me, just as if we were going to San Vicente to buy flour."

Though he hadn't thought much about it since digging it out of the yard, the ninety-one dollars—seventy-five of it for Gutierrez—suddenly seemed heavy and hot in his pants pocket. He dropped a hand to cover it, thinking what a catastrophe it would be if he lost it. Or if someone took it from him.

Walking, not slow, not fast, Jose went on until he saw the lights of the border station. At that point, he looked up at the street sign, checked the map again, and made a sharp left turn, going down a dirt street. Within two blocks, the houses began to be scattered, and the lights faded out.

Once, a car came up behind them, and Jose said to himself, just look at it, wave, and keep walking. His heart hammered as the headlights washed over them.

Aside from his breathing, and the slither of his feet over the loose dust and sand of the road, there were only night sounds. Crickets and frogs dinned in the nearby irrigation ditch that paralleled the road. It was warm, and Jose felt his shirt begin to get wet.

Sanchez kept easy pace, his big head rotating from side to side, nose sniffing.

In a few minutes, Jose stopped to study a concrete kilometer marker. He said quietly to Sanchez, "Now, we must cross the field."

He guessed the field was about half a kilometer wide. Trotting, occasionally looking back, he moved in a straight line through the knee-high weeds. Sanchez bounded almost soundlessly beside him.

When they reached the road, Jose stopped and squatted in the weeds that flanked it. The lights of Tecate were over his shoulders to the left. Now and then, faint sounds drifted through. Music and the honk of horns.

After he'd caught his breath, he whispered, "Okay, Sanchez," and they were off again.

In a moment, Jose could see the high fence and said, "Stop, Sanchez." He made out the dark mass of reeds against the bottom of the fence. That had to be the spot.

"Come," he whispered and began to crawl. Sanchez seemed puzzled that Jose was traveling on all fours and kept bumping him. It took less than two minutes to reach the fence. He started to touch it but then remembered hearing that sometimes the fences were wired for alarm.

On his knees in the damp earth of the drainway, he carefully parted the reeds and saw the open space, about two square feet beneath the fence. He whispered to Sanchez, "Go through."

The dog stared at him, stumpy tail flagging.

"Go through," Jose repeated.

Sanchez sat down, panting heavily, his tongue out and dripping. He looked at Jose as if this were a rest time during a game.

Jose snorted with frustration and decided he'd have to go under first. He started through but found himself almost crushed in the narrow entry when Sanchez piled in beside him, like a playful hippo.

And then they were in the *Estados Unidos*.

34

It was all so simple.

The American road was less than a kilometer away, and Jose stayed on his knees to look and listen. His dark face glistened with sweat. He made the sign of the cross and rose to a crouch, whispering, "Okay, Sanchez."

They plunged on toward the road, stopping only when the headlights of a car lifted to spray the whole area with light. Jose flattened to the ground.

Before going on again, Jose straightened up and looked both ways. Then he nodded off to the left. They angled that way, and Jose soon saw Gutierrez standing out in front of the raised hood, as if the Chevy were in trouble. The lights were on.

A truck roared by, stirring the warm air, trailing exhaust.

Jose stopped and crouched again. As the diesel noise subsided, he said softly, "*Señor* Gutierrez."

The *pocho* did not even look up. His hands were down in the engine. But Jose heard his voice. "Move quickly. The trunk is open. Get in it."

They raced for the back of the car. Jose whipped the lid up and crawled in, kneeling on the blanket Gutierrez had put down. Then he sprawled out on his side. There was plenty of room.

Sanchez hesitated, puzzled. He was standing by the bumper looking suspicious. Suddenly he began yelping.

"Shut him up," Gutierrez snarled.

"Get in," Jose told the dog.

Sanchez finally leaped up, and Jose pulled the lid down, closing out the stars.

Sanchez was still confused and frightened. He began to thump around like a calf in a stock run, banging against Jose; trying to stand up. Enrique was right. Sanchez was insane. Punching him hard on a flank, Jose said, angrily, "Settle down."

Up front, Gutierrez slammed the hood. He walked to the back, lifted the trunk lid, looked in, and banged it shut, saying nothing.

Jose heard the car start and put his arm around Sanchez's neck. His throat felt as dry as the dust on the road to Enrique's.

6

THE INSIDE OF THE TRUNK smelled of exhaust fumes and rubber and metal. And, more and more, of Sanchez.

The wheel by Jose's ear whined, and there was a steady roar from the tailpipe beneath him. He felt like an eel stuffed into a dark bottle. He was curled up against the right-hand side of the car, his head on the shelf-like base that usually held the spare tire.

Sanchez was cramped against the other side, his paws extending to Jose's belly. He seemed resigned now and had stopped moving around.

The old car roared on, slowing now and then for curves. There was plenty of air in the trunk when it moved fast but about twenty minutes after they'd started, Gutierrez put on the brakes for a stop sign. The fumes became thick, and Jose closed his mouth and held his nose. Sanchez sneezed several times.

A while later, there was another stop, and then Jose felt the car make a sharp turn. He whispered to Sanchez, "I think we're headed north."

He wished there was a crack so that he could see out. It was a shame to have the tires flying over this new country and not be able to see it. He wondered when Gutierrez would let them sit up front.

Soon, the constant drone from the tailpipe caused him to drift off to sleep.

It was early in the morning when Gutierrez finally stopped and got out of the car, awakening Jose. For a moment, panic hit him. He wondered if the patrol had stopped Gutierrez, but he heard no voices.

Then the key turned in the lock, and fresh air rushed in. Jose blinked up at Gutierrez, and Sanchez rose to his feet, shaking his head.

The *pocho* was smiling. "Good morning," he said. "It's safe now. You can ride up front."

Jose crawled out of the trunk, Sanchez leaping ahead of him. He did not realize how stiff he was until his feet touched the ground. He worked his legs and arms while Sanchez' body lengthened in a stretch that seemed to go forever.

"It was hard to tell my elbow from my knee in there," he said.

Sanchez lifted his leg on Gutierrez' back tire. The *pocho* grunted with annoyance but then said, "Well, I guess that's a good idea."

For a moment, they breathed in the crisp mountain air. It was barely light; cold, damp, and misty. Jose looked around at the scrub trees. The road was deserted and ghostly.

"We better go," Gutierrez said.

As Gutierrez pulled away, he handed a small thermos to Jose, along with a bag containing tortillas and white cheese. Jose filled a cup with hot milk and drank it. Then he put some cheese between two cold tortillas. He passed some cheese back to Sanchez, reminding himself to get Sanchez water when they stopped for gas.

His mouth full of cheese and tortilla, Jose asked, "Where will we go after we find my father?"

"San Ramon, in the Salinas Valley."

It meant nothing to Jose, but he was glad it had a Spanish name. Perhaps there would be a lot of people who spoke Spanish up there. "My father will work there?"

Gutierrez nodded. "There are many people from Mexico working on the ranches and in the fields."

"Will they be like us?"

Eyes narrowing, Gutierrez glanced over. "You mean wetbacks? Yes, some will be."

"How did we get that name?" Jose asked. "It's a bad name." So was the Spanish name, *alambristo*—fence jumper.

Gutierrez chuckled but kept his eyes on the road. "What's a name? A long time ago Mexicans swam the rivers and canals to cross the border. Some still do. That's how they got the name. I think it came from Texas. But don't let it bother you. We are helping them. Americans do not like to work the fields."

Jose thought about that for a while and then said, "You know, I can't speak much English."

"You'll learn," Gutierrez said. "Have your father buy a small radio. That's the way I learned thirty years ago. It will be much easier for you. Old people have a problem."

"I hope it is easy," Jose said, yawning.

At sunrise, they reached Elsinore and started down the mountain slope toward San Juan Capistrano. Jose, who had been dozing, awakened before they arrived at the village and asked about the mission. He'd heard a story about millions of swallows living there.

Gutierrez said, "It's just ahead, but I don't think we should stop. Our luck is good. Let's keep it that way."

Jose agreed.

"Someday you can come back and see it."

"Yes."

Finally, they came to the Santa Ana Freeway and headed north. Jose began watching everything.

Beside the freeway, the fields were lush and green, though the low grass mountains, farther back, were brown from summer heat. There were miles of orange groves; great fields that made their own field at Colnett look as if it could be held in a hand.

Soon, houses began to appear on either side of the

freeway; hundreds of them. Jose was stunned by their number.

"Many have swimming pools," Gutierrez said. "Just wait. These are only the poor people."

"With swimming pools?" Jose was certain it was a joke.

Gutierrez laughed. "I have a real treat for you. We will pass Disneyland in about a half hour. You know of that place?"

Jose had read about it, and Fernando had been up there. That's all he'd bragged about for weeks. Jose wished Gutierrez would volunteer to stop so they could have a better look. But he didn't mention it.

His head swiveled from side to side as they passed house after house tucked against the freeway. Unlike at Colnett, the neighbors were close enough to call over to each other; maybe to hear each other cough. There would never be a problem of having someone to talk to.

"I did not know about this," Jose said, and Gutierrez grinned over at him, taking pleasure from his excitement.

And cars! Everyone owned a car. It was incredible. It was rush hour, and there seemed to be thousands of them. Most of them looked new; not covered with mud and dust, not patched up, Jose noticed.

Then the alp of Disneyland loomed on the left. "There," Gutierrez said, stealing a glance at the wide eyes and open mouth.

It was exactly like the pictures Jose had seen in the comic book at the San Vicente store. It was just as Fernando had described it. He could imagine what lay beyond that alp. There was a train that ran on a single rail, and a riverboat in a man-made lake, and a rocket and a pirate's den. He got up on his hands and knees so he could look past the back of Gutierrez's head.

"Disneyland, Sanchez," he said, pointing, but the dog was digging beneath a scarred ear with a hind paw, paying no attention.

The skyline of Los Angeles rose and fell, and they went by other towns solidly against each other for more than an hour. They stopped for gas in one, and Jose got water for Sanchez.

Rolling again, they were in ranchlands. By the time they reached the outskirts of Oxnard, Jose's eyes were bleary. Cabo Colnett and its lonely silence was on another planet, and he did not care if he ever saw it again.

Although Jose could hardly wait to meet his father, he was concerned about Sanchez. The last few miles he'd thought of how best to do it—keep Sanchez well hidden in the back seat until he'd greeted his father? Or maybe let Sanchez bound out ahead of him, wag that chopped-off tail, and jump up on Maldonado, as usual. Either way, it was a problem. He hoped his father would be in a good mood.

Gutierrez headed for a long, tin-roofed shed by a railroad spur track. Jose could see boxes of carrots on the platform. There were also hampers that looked as if they might hold beans. They were being loaded into trucks.

At the far end was an office building. A number of men were standing around outside. Some were Mexican, Jose noticed. They wore straw hats, white shirts, jeans, and heavy shoes, much as Maldonado usually did. But Jose could not spot his father.

Gutierrez stopped and looked around. "He said he'd meet us here. By the loading dock for Consolidated Farms."

"It's a busy place," Jose said anxiously.

"Stay in the car," Gutierrez said. "I'll find him." He got out and went into the office building.

Sanchez had poked his head out of the back window and was sniffing the countryside. There was a smell of liquid fertilizer in the air. Jose said to him, "You act like you're happy to see him, eh? Wag your tail."

Jose was tempted to get out and ask some of the men around the office building if they knew Maldonado, from Cabo Colnett. He didn't recognize any of them, but he thought they might have met Maldonado in the fields.

Then he saw Gutierrez pounding down the short flight of steps from the office. His face was grim.

Gutierrez slid back into the car and shut the door with a bang. He slapped the steering wheel. "Your father isn't here."

"Where is he?"

"About a hundred fifty miles away by now. A crop needed picking. They were short-handed, so they took him over there this morning."

Jose didn't know what to say.

"He left a message with the bus dispatcher."

"Did he have to go?"

Gutierrez glanced over. "Yes." He saw the look of disappointment and fright on Jose's face.

"Jose, your father is not legal and these men know it. They know they can tell him what to do and where to go. If he causes trouble, they get rid of him and then let Immigration know. Besides, he's up here to earn money. He needs the work."

"What did the message say?"

"He wants me to take you on to San Ramon. He'll join you there in about ten days, when they finish the picking."

Jose was alarmed at the thought of being alone for ten days in a strange place. In Colnett, it was bad enough. "Where will I stay?"

Gutierrez turned the key. "Haines's Farm. You'll both be working there. I'll talk to Eduardo. He won't like it, but what can I do?" He turned the car in a tight circle.

Out on the road again, heading north, he said, "It'll be all right, Jose. I just wish you didn't have this damn dog along. Eddie wasn't even expecting you, much less a dog."

"Maybe I should go to my father."

Gutierrez shook his head. "That would be worse, where he is. At least I know Eddie."

They drove in silence until finally Gutierrez cooled down. "You just mind your business up there, and make that dog behave, huh? It'll be all right. Haines has the best labor camp in California. Some are sewers."

Jose nodded and took to watching the country again. Now and then, they saw the ocean. They passed oil wells and went through a large town, and then they were in farmland again.

7

ALMOST THREE HOURS LATER, the Chevrolet came down off the new freeway ramp, and Jose saw the village of San Ramon.

Gutierrez said, "It isn't much."

Jose thought it looked magnificent. It was twenty times the size of San Vicente. Its main street was paved. There were stores and a post office. There was a big mission and church. There was a railroad crossing and even streetlights. Gutierrez was spoiled, he thought.

They headed east over a dirt road toward Haines's Bright-Pack Farm.

"What do we do about Sanchez?" Jose asked, a bit nervously.

"Let him stay in the back seat until I talk to Eddie. Keep him quiet."

In a few minutes, they drove through the Haines's gate. It was a giant farm, with many buildings and much equipment. There were a half-dozen big tractor trailers parked not far inside the fence, each with massive painted tomatoes and heads of lettuce on the sides.

Gutierrez stopped the car about a hundred feet from the small office building. Dropping his chubby hands into his lap, he took a deep breath. "All right, we're here. I'll take the rest of the money now."

Jose hesitated. "I was to give this to my father to give to you."

"But your father isn't here."

Jose nodded. With his back to Gutierrez, he dug into his pocket and counted out the final seventy-five dollars. It seemed like a lot of money for so short a trip. Nineteen dollars was left, and he planned to give this to his father. He handed the fee to Gutierrez.

The *pocho* folded it and said, "Now, let's go see Eduardo. He's the No. 2 foreman. You let me do the talking."

Jose pulled the fiber suitcase out from beside the dog.

Gutierrez went into the office and came back out with Eddie, who looked about the same age as Maldonado. He had a thin mustache and clipped hair. They moved to one side of the office building and paused.

Jose was puzzled when he saw Gutierrez pass over some of the money to Eddie. It looked as if he was counting out almost half of it. Eddie said something and nodded. Then they walked over to Jose.

"You didn't say anything about a boy last week, Gutierrez."

Gutierrez seemed apprehensive. "He is strong, and he knows farm work." They spoke in Spanish.

Eddie was very businesslike. "How old is he?" he asked, as if Jose were not even there.

Jose started to reply but Gutierrez said quickly, "Fourteen."

Jose frowned but decided to keep his mouth shut.

Eddie blew a breath out. "All we need is problems with the labor people. When will his father arrive?"

"In ten days."

"I don't know, Gutierrez. Maybe you should take him back."

"I can't do that."

Jose found himself disliking Eduardo already. He had thought the foreman would greet him the way people in Baja did, but the man hadn't even spoken to him.

"Please, Eduardo, we have done business before. We'll do it again."

"I will work very hard," Jose said. "And my father always works hard."

Eddie shrugged and said half-heartedly, "All right, come on."

They followed Eddie into the small office. Inside was a counter and behind it several desks. At one, a burly man in shirt sleeves was working over long pieces of paper.

Gutierrez whispered, "That is *Señor* Klosterman, the farm manager. But you deal with Eddie. Tell your father."

There was a younger man filling out papers at the

counter. He nodded and smiled. Jose smiled back. From the way he was dressed he looked like a *pocho* with money.

Eddie ducked behind the counter and pushed some forms across. "You're sixteen if anyone asks. Got that? Write it down. You live over in San Ardo. U.S. citizen."

"Yes, *señor*," Jose replied. It seemed that in this whole trip nothing was truthful.

"Sign them," Gutierrez said.

Jose saw that they were written in Spanish and English. "What are they?" he whispered.

"Never mind. Work permit and health card. There, on those lines." Gutierrez seemed anxious to leave.

Jose signed the papers without reading them.

The young *pocho* glanced over, frowning at Gutierrez. He had curly hair and a neat mustache. His face was strong and confident.

Eddie reached for the papers, saying, "Seventy-five cents an hour. Your food will be a dollar seventy-five cents a day."

That was a lot of money for food, Jose thought. In Colnett, he could eat for a week on that.

He saw that the young man was still frowning at Gutierrez. Sweat had broken out on Gutierrez's forehead.

Eddie went on. "We'll put you in a cabin. They'd make a soccer ball out of you in the barracks."

Jose did not understand. "Soccer ball?"

"Nothing but bums and winos in the barracks," Eddie said.

49

The young man spoke to Jose. "You alone?"

"Yes, *señor*. But my father will be here soon."

The young man looked at Eddie. "I think it might be safer if he stayed with me."

Jose felt better. The *pocho* seemed nice.

Eddie shrugged. "I don't care."

"My name is Giron. Rafael Giron." He extended a hand to Jose. "Share my cabin until your father arrives."

"Yes, *señor*."

"What's your name?"

"Jose Maldonado Alvarez."

Giron smiled. "Okay, Jose. We'll do this together. This is my first day here, too." He spoke to Eddie in English.

"Take Cabin 6," Eddie answered. "Morning meal at 6:30; evening between 5:30 and 7. Bus leaves here every morning except Sunday at seven o'clock. Don't miss it. And remember what I told you, boy. Sixteen. Sixteen. Sixteen."

Jose nodded.

Giron said, "Let's go."

Outside, Giron asked Gutierrez sharply, "Why are they paying Jose seventy-five cents an hour when I get a dollar and a quarter?"

Gutierrez reddened. "It is part of the arrangement."

Giron looked at him with contempt.

"Quick," Gutierrez said, "get the dog. I want to leave."

Giron glanced over at the car. "A dog?"

Jose swallowed. "Yes, *señor*. Do you mind?"

Giron laughed weakly. "I guess not."

Jose ran to open the door, and Sanchez bounded out, almost bowling him over, his stump of tail whipping.

Gutierrez climbed in, taking a quick look toward the office. "Good-bye, Jose," he said. "Good luck."

Giron snapped, "Get going."

The old Chevy left in a hurry.

8

THERE WERE TWO BUNKS in each of the white-painted cabins, which strung out in a double row from the three barracks buildings, and the shower and toilet building. The paint was browning from age. Pepper trees were dotted around nearby.

The mattresses looked as if they had been dragged through the dust. Two gray blankets were folded at the bottom of each bunk. A naked, fly-specked bulb hung from the ceiling over a rickety table. There were two wooden chairs. A calendar from Mexicali hung on one wall at the far end. Days had been marked off as if the occupant had looked forward to leaving.

"It's very nice," Jose said, although it did smell stale.

Giron knelt down by the mattresses and began poking a finger into the seams. "I'm looking for lice," he said. "In a few days, I'll buy something and spray them."

Jose began to unpack. There were wooden pegs for

clothes on each wall. Giron said, "We can fix this up a bit. I'll borrow a broom and find a rag to dust."

Jose turned to look at him. His way of talking was strange. "You are not a field worker," he said.

"No, Jose. I'm a teacher."

Jose was impressed. This meant Giron had gone to college.

"I teach grammar school in East Los Angeles, but I'm working on my master's thesis. I'm doing research this summer. On migrant workers. People like you."

"What is a thesis?"

"It's like a book. Like a long report you do in school. Then I'll get another degree."

"But you should not be here," Jose said. "A teacher picking crops."

"For a reason," Giron answered.

"Does Eduardo know you are a teacher?"

"No," Giron said. "And let's don't tell him."

Jose shook his head. "No one seems to tell the truth up here."

Giron laughed softly. "You are wise. But sometimes it is best not to tell the truth. For me, it is now. Okay?"

Jose nodded and went on unpacking. He removed his straw crucifix from the suitcase and hung it on a nail near the foot of his bunk. He stripped out everything except the sharp kitchen knife with the deer-horn handle on it. He left that in the suitcase.

At about five-thirty, the buses returned from the fields

and several hundred men poured out. Jose saw that they were mostly Mexican, but there were a few blacks and a few whites. He sat on the steps of No. 6 with Sanchez and watched while the workers went off to the barracks buildings, talking and laughing, then began filling the shower and toilet buildings.

They looked no different than other men he had seen.

About six o'clock, Jose and Giron went to the evening meal in the long, noisy mess hall with its wooden tables and heavy white chinaware. The food wasn't like what he usually had in Colnett, but it was good. Pan-fried steaks, potatoes, green beans, yellow pudding, and a pink-colored juice that didn't taste much like anything.

He sat close to Giron. There was a jabber of conversation around the room and a lot of laughter. Several of the men looked at them but said nothing.

Jose cut off half his steak and wrapped it in a paper napkin for Sanchez but Giron said, "Maybe we can make a deal with the cook. We'll go to the kitchen later. From the looks of Sanchez, he'd down that in one bite."

"He does eat a lot," Jose admitted. That was one thing neither he nor Enrique had considered.

Well after dark, Jose finished his prayers before the straw crucifix, and lay down on the thin mattress. He thought about getting up again to place the horn knife by his side, but decided that was silly. Sanchez was two feet away and Giron was there, writing in a notebook, beneath the dim light of the naked bulb.

Jose wanted to talk but waited until Giron had finished and had come back from the toilet. Then he said, "You were born in this country?"

"Yes, East Los Angeles. But my parents were born in Sonora."

"You are fortunate," Jose said.

"Maybe."

Giron took his clothes off, latched the screen door, and turned off the lights.

"I don't know much about Americans," Jose said.

"What do you know about them?"

"Well, they come past our adobe in trucks or trailers. Sometimes, I wait a while and then follow them. There is a good camping spot about half a mile south of Enrique's, and they often spend a few days there."

"Who is Enrique?"

"A friend of ours. He fishes."

"Um-huh."

"I go near to them—but not too near—and sit down. If they are friendly and wave, I go on up. Those trailers are something. Beds, an ice box, a stove, a toilet, a sink. They are better than most of the houses in Baja."

"I suppose so," said Giron.

"A little while ago one family came with a pickup towing a trailer. They had two motorcycles. A large one for the father. A small one for the boy. He wasn't even as old as I am. They took the motorcycles down and put on red helmets. The boy's helmet looked exactly like the father's."

Giron looked through the shadows at Jose. "Go on."

"The rest of the day they went up and down the trail on the bluff. They never smiled at all. The father's motorcycle threw dirt. *Brrrrrrrr-rummmmmmmmm zzzzzzzzzzeeeeeddinn.* The boy's motorcycle had a *put-put-put-put-put* sound. They only stopped to gas up."

Jose paused. "I wanted to ride, too. Sometimes the boy would come near me and wave, but he never offered a ride. Funny. The wife and daughter sat down at the beach all day under an umbrella. It seemed strange that the father and son had come so far just to ride their motorcycles. They didn't fish or swim or play ball or even look at big Colnett. Just *brrrrrrrrrrrr-rummmmmmmmmmm zzzzzzeeedddin* and *put-put-put-put-put-put.*"

Giron smiled. In the darkness he could see the outline of the small figure on the opposite bunk.

"Late that afternoon I went home and fed the stock, but I came back again after the sun was down. They were all in the trailer, and the lights were on. The mother and father were shouting at each other. Then the father hit the daughter."

"What did you do then?" asked Giron.

"I went home. I could hear shouts from the trailer all the way back. I wanted the boy's motorbike, but I was glad I had my own father."

Giron said quietly, "Not all Americans are like that."

"I know. There was another family that invited me in for a Coke. Before they left, they gave me an old bicycle.

It had a bad tire, but it rode well. Just last week I gave it to our Camalu cousin. They have many children in that house."

"That was kind of you, Jose," Giron said. "What does your father think about the Americans?"

Jose thought a moment. "He has never said too much about them. Neither has Enrique. Oh, they joke about all their money, but I have seen how they act around them."

"How do they act?"

"Different from the men in Ensenada. When Enrique wants to sell the tourists a *langosta* he never walks up to the trailers. He just passes by with a wet sack, carrying one in his hand. Always, the tourists will shout over to him. Then he goes up."

"And your father?"

"When my father needs money he might walk along the road with some corn. Or go by their camp with a bucket of clams, letting a few spill out. He never even looks at them until they yell."

Giron laughed softly.

"My father says it is a matter of pride. He says that in the city, people lose their pride quickly."

After a moment, Giron said, "I agree."

A train passed by about nine-thirty. Although the tracks were almost a kilometer from Haines's Main, the cabin shook, and Jose awakened with a start. He heard the rumble and felt the cabin shaking.

"It's a train, that's all," Giron said quietly.

Jose looked over. Giron was staring up at the ceiling.

Jose tried to make himself comfortable again. In Colnett there were no trains. At night, there was no sound except the wind in the trees and the animal noises.

Sometime in the middle of the night, Jose reawakened when there was a noise outside. Sanchez was up, growling deep in his belly.

Giron sat up. "Just another dog," he said.

9

AFTER BREAKFAST, Jose said to Sanchez, "You must stay here today while I work. Not bark or cause trouble. And don't step in your water pan. Understand?"

Sanchez was sitting in the middle of the cabin, paws planted, big jaws open. He appeared to be listening, but he was ready and anxious to go wherever they went.

"Do not cause *Señor* Eddie to come down here," Jose warned. "Listen to me."

Giron, who was standing nearby, said, "I don't think I've ever seen a dog like that. He looks like a cross between a bear, a dog, and a bundle of old rugs. What's wrong with his eyes? One's green. The other one's brown."

"Nothing wrong with them. That's just the way he was made."

Giron shrugged. "It's time to go."

They started for the door, and Sanchez abruptly rose. Jose said, "Guard! Sanchez," and went out quickly.

There were a few low moans and then silence as they went on to the bus.

Stooped backs dotted the green fields, and there were splotches of deep red where fifty-pound lugs were being filled with Haines Bright-Pack tomatoes. The tomatoes were large and juicy, Jose noted. Much larger than anything his father had been able to grow in Colnett. And the earth was black and moist from continuous irrigation.

They picked steadily and quietly. A flat-bed truck idled nearby, now and then moving behind them as they advanced up the rows. Jose felt good. It had been gray when the bus turned into No. 4 field, but now the sun was out, warming his back and making his muscles supple.

There were about forty workers in the field, including six or eight women. Giron said, "The women are local people, I think. The men are mostly migrant workers."

"Illegal?"

"Some, maybe. They go from farm to farm."

Around ten o'clock, one of the younger Mexicans, or maybe he was a *pocho*, said to Jose, "Slow down."

Jose straightened up. "This is the only way I know how to work, *señor*."

The man's eyes held a warning. "There won't be any work if you keep going that fast. Slow down."

Giron said quietly to Jose, "Go slower. Don't cause any trouble."

They bent again. Jose was a little confused. The tomatoes were there; the lugs were there. They should be filled rapidly. Perhaps the rules were different up here. He went at a slower pace.

Once, taking a lug to the truck, he passed an *americano,* a flabby man working at the end of a row. The man straightened up, grinned, and winked.

Jose smiled and kept on walking.

When he returned, the man said, *"Bueno, bueno!"*

Jose nodded and smiled, going back to Giron's side.

A third time, as Jose passed, the man whinneyed like a horse and clacked his false teeth.

Jose felt uncomfortable and hurried away.

At noon, the food truck came out from Haines Main. They got soup in a paper container; rice and beans and beef slivers. The truck left a metal container of coffee and a box of oranges, then moved on to another field.

They ate in the shade of the bus, their backs against the muddy rear wheel. All morning, the pickers had been mostly silent, but there was much talk now. A worn, gray-haired Mexican sat near them. Giron was complaining loudly about the conditions at Haines Main.

"It is heaven," the old Mexican said in Spanish. "In the old days, migrant families slept in their cars. I've seen babies suffocate in the heat near El Centro. I've felt cockroaches run across my face at night. I've eaten slop for days on end. This place is heaven. You can take a bath at night, and there is a toilet here in the fields. You don't know."

Jose noticed that some of the pickers were staring at Giron. One finally said, "There's a lot you college boys don't know."

Giron remained silent.

"It is a game you play, but you don't know you play it. It is only when you have to pay the money to eat and sleep and feed others that you understand it isn't a game," the old man went on.

Jose felt badly for Giron, and wondered why he didn't tell them he was a teacher; an important man.

When the workers began talking about something else, Jose whispered, "How did they know you were from college?"

"My hands, I suppose, or the way I talk."

Jose glanced at Giron's hands for the first time. They were not the hands of a farmer. Not like Maldonado's or Enrique's. They weren't even calloused and nicked.

Giron said, "I did it on purpose. I wanted to hear what the old man would say."

But in the cabin that evening, Giron said, "I must be more careful."

"Why?"

"The Mexicans and Chicanos suspect that I do not need to do this, and the *americano* workers have always resented us. They'll all be on my back."

"I don't understand," said Jose.

"When they had the *bracero* program, the Mexicans were under government control. Sometimes they got more money than Americans for the same work. Even the people in the towns did not like the *braceros,* I hear. They spent very little. They sent most of their money home. Before that, the Mexicans always worked cheaper. Okay?"

"Okay."

"You know Eddie is cheating you, don't you?"

"No."

"He's taking fifty cents an hour from you. Maybe he's splitting it with Klosterman. You're not getting full pay, Jose. Neither will your father. It's one reason I'm writing about this."

Jose nodded thoughtfully. "Yesterday I saw Gutierrez give Eddie some of our money." It had been bothering him.

"I'm not surprised," Giron said. "They have a deal, I expect. You know how I got this cabin? Paid Eddie ten dollars."

Jose frowned. It all seemed so complicated up here. Why should there be deals? They were all earning wages. Still puzzled, he asked Giron.

Giron laughed hollowly. "People! Makes no difference whether you're Mexican or American, Jose. They do things mostly for themselves. For profit."

That had not really occurred to Jose. His father and Enrique seemed to do very little for themselves, aside from taking good care to feed their stomachs and having a few beers. He thought about it for a moment, deciding it was too large a thing to figure out all at once.

He got his towel and with Sanchez tagging along, went to the shower. He had never taken a hot shower, and he was looking forward to it. His father had rigged a cold one at Colnett with an oil drum, but most of the summer baths he had taken in a tin tub in the yard. In the winter months, he'd taken them on the floor of the adobe, his father or mother pouring in steaming water from a kettle.

On the steps of the oval-roofed, corrugated iron building, he ordered Sanchez to stay and went inside. It smelled of strong disinfectant mixed with sweat and steam. There were toilet stalls at one end of the building, near the door, and shaving basins and mirrors along one wall. In the center of the room was a long wooden bench on which to park clothing, shoes, and towels. Most of the men had gone, but a few were still coming in. A few were under the showers.

Jose put his soap and towel on an empty space on the bench. At the far end, the heavy-set *americano* picker was peeling down. His flabby body was the color of flour except for the vee at his neck, which was mahogany colored, as was his face. From his elbows down, his arms, too, were mahogany. He looked painted.

Eyeing Jose, he yelled, "Hey, we got the new one tonight."

Jose did not understand what he was saying and turned his head the other way, feeling self-conscious.

The *americano* said, "He's pretty. He looks tender."

Jose heard some of the men laughing. Taking his shirt off, he felt crimson rising under his cheeks.

The *americano* laughed. "Not so tender at all, now that I see him. He's got mus-culls."

Jose wondered whether or not he should leave. Something about the way the man was talking did not seem right. But he slipped his jeans off, tossing them beside his shirt.

There was a whistle, "Whew-whew!" As he stripped on down, the whistle went, "Whew-whew-wheeeeeee . . ."

There were about ten open nozzles spraying into soap-slicked drains. The last nozzle wasn't being used, and Jose went over to it quickly, glancing up to see that the flabby man had moved to the next one.

"What's your name, boy?" he asked, reaching over to twist a valve.

Jose thought he understood but said nothing. This man with the soft face and double chin made him ill. He ignored him as the hot water began to spray. He scrubbed and then turned to let the water slam into his face.

The *americano* shouted, "You not very friendly, boy."

Jose felt a hand grasp his shoulder and wondered if he should shout for Sanchez. The hand held him firmly. Moving out of the stream of water, he said, "Please, *señor.*"

The man grinned. "I jus' want you an' I to be friendly."

The hand began to press. There was something

strange and terrible about this man, and Jose tried to pull his shoulder away.

"Jus' relax."

Jose could stand it no longer. Without thinking about what he was doing, he scooped scum off the soap tray and flung it into the man's eyes.

The *americano* screamed and wiped at his face, then drew back an open palm, cursing wildly.

A voice cut through the shower room, speaking in English. It was like a whip pop, and Jose looked over to see a strapping man about six nozzles down with his finger pointed their way. White suds cascaded over his naked black body. His eyes were glaring.

Surprised, the flabby man dropped his hand. Finally, he turned the shower off and waddled back down the bench line. The black man spoke sharply as he passed, his finger forking out like an ebony arrow.

Heart drumming, now understanding what Eddie meant about the "soccer ball," Jose finished his shower without looking toward the far end of the room. As he was drying off, the black man came up, mopping himself with a towel. He said, "Watch that one, kid. He's nothin' but evil." Jose did not fully understand, but recognized the word *evil*, for the black man added, "*Malo. Muy malo.*"

Jose said, "*Muchas gracias, señor.*" He dressed quickly and got Sanchez. As he began walking down the dirt lane between the cabins, he met Giron, who was headed for the bath with his cake of soap and towel. He started to tell the teacher but decided not to. There might be more trouble. He might be kicked off the farm and that would mean Maldonado couldn't work.

Giron grinned. "Makes you feel good, huh?"

"Yes, *señor*," Jose replied and went on to No. 6.

During the evening meal, Jose noticed that the *americano* was glancing at him now and then, but he kept his eyes on his plate, or on other things.

In the twilight, he took Sanchez for a long run in the newly plowed field east of Haines Main, hoping that his father would soon arrive. Maldonado could snap the flabby man like a bean.

Back in the cabin, while Giron wrote in his notebook, Jose took the stub of pencil from his suitcase and on the back of a small box he'd retrieved from behind the kitchen began sketching the field workers picking tomatoes. He sat on the edge of the bed, holding the box on his knees.

Soon, Giron looked over. Then he got up and stood by Jose. "I didn't know you could do this," he said. "That's marvelous."

"It is nothing. Without color, you cannot see the green of the fields or the red of the tomatoes."

"But you have the feeling. That's the way it looked today. Have you had art lessons?"

"No, *señor*."

"It's remarkable. You have a lot of talent."

Feeling very pleased, Jose went back to work on it.

In bed, Giron said, "I'm surprised your father didn't try to call here tonight."

"He knows that I am okay."

"How does he know that?"

Jose was silent for a moment, then said, "My father was a man when he was a boy, and I guess he thinks I am that way, too."

"Are you?"

"No."

"You seem to do all right."

Then Jose told Giron something he'd never told anyone else. "I love my father, but I don't like him. Do you understand?"

"Hmh."

"Do you understand?"

"I suppose so. I've just never heard it put that way."

Jose talked about Maldonado for a while, and then Giron talked about his father. Jose learned that Giron was from a big family and that they lived in the barrio in East Los Angeles. Giron's father was a tile setter, and one of Giron's brothers and one of his sisters had gone to college, too.

Jose fell asleep thinking enviously about the large Giron family, and wondering where his father was; what he was doing.

10

THERE WAS NO ONE else of Jose's age in the labor camp, but he'd noticed that there were some young people in several houses about a half kilometer away. Giron had said that these were foremen homes. They were roomy and neat. New cars or trucks were usually parked around them.

At one house Jose had spotted a red-haired boy who looked about thirteen. There was also a pale, blond girl who might be eleven or twelve at the same house. Although they probably did not speak Spanish, he thought he might talk to them the way he'd talked to some of the *turistas* at Colnett. Pointing, saying a word or two in English.

He discussed it with Giron. The teacher said, "Why not? You should make friends here. But I wouldn't tell them about crawling under that fence."

Jose laughed. "I wouldn't know how to tell them in English."

The next night, Friday, he decided how he'd do it. He couldn't just walk up and say, "We *amigo*, eh?" It was better to do something like his father and Enrique did at Colnett.

On Saturday morning he began collecting horseflies, selecting the big ones that zoomed around the fields, drawn by the fertilized earth. He placed them in a plastic vial he'd found the previous year on the beach below Melings. Tiny air holes were punched into the top.

Giron came by just as he grabbed one. "What in the world are you doing?"

"Catching flies, of course." Jose laughed, shoving a fly into the vial.

"Oh? Well, that's a hobby I've never heard of." Shaking his head, Giron rested his full lug of Bright-Packs. "What do you do with them?"

"I'll show you some time," Jose replied, pleased with himself.

They knocked off at noon, as scheduled, and went back to Haines Main for lunch. After eating, Giron said he wanted to go into town. He needed the lice spray and a new toothbrush, and joked about getting some perfume for Sanchez. Jose asked if he could go along, and took a dollar of the Colnett money from the hiding place under his mattress. He did not think his father would mind, now that he was earning a wage.

In San Ramon, Giron made his purchases, and Jose bought a tube of quick-drying glue. When they returned to the labor camp, it was practically deserted. Some of the men were sleeping. Others were playing horseshoes or checkers beneath the pepper trees. Still others had gone into town to drink beer or wine in the Spanish cafe. It was a warm, lazy afternoon.

Giron began playing checkers with the man next door. From beneath the bunk Jose took a small balsa glider that he'd bought in Ensenada. He stuck the glue into his pocket, checked the flies to see if they were still strong, and headed for the foremen houses. Sanchez followed.

He spotted the boy out in the side yard, working on his bike. It was saddle-down, and the chain was off the sprocket. Jose hesitated a moment, then went into the open field beside the house. Stealing a glance, he saw that the boy was staring at him.

He inserted the wing into the glider, then the rudder and tail fins. He tested it with a shallow arc, and it glided smoothly back to the ground. Then he took the glue out and uncapped it, feeling the boy's eyes still on him.

He opened the vial, extracted a horsefly bigger than a bumblebee but not as fat, and put a spot of the fast-setting glue on its belly, pushing it down midway on the glider's wing. He blew on it.

By this time, he was almost certain the boy was walking toward him. He waited a moment, then released the glider. It rose in the air on angry wings.

Jose heard a voice speaking in English just behind him. "Hey, where'd you learn to do that?" He did not understand the words but knew that they formed a question.

Grinning, he turned. "Hi, *amigo*."

The glider zoomed crazily through the air, and the red-haired boy laughed. "Wow," he yelled. He had freckles and a wide mouth. There were wire braces on his teeth.

As usual, the fly eventually loosened itself and took off like a frightened midget quail. The glider came slowly back to earth, landing perfectly on its spar.

Jose shook the vial and held it up, nodding toward the glider. The boy grinned and ran for it. When he came back, Jose passed him the glue and motioned for him to try it.

"Who taught you that?" the boy asked. "I've never seen that before."

Jose thought he understood but didn't know how to explain. There weren't many things to do at Cabo Colnett, so you invented things that cost little money. Flies were free. Glue wasn't much. If you were careful, a glider lasted hundreds of flights.

"I'm Michael. Mike," the boy said.

That translated to Miguel, Jose was certain.

Jose tapped his chest. "Jose Maldonado. Joe."

The boy examined the raging flies.

Jose said, "You, Miguel. Fly. Fly." He made an airplane motion with his hands.

They made eight more flights and then fixed the bike chain. Finally they went inside. Jose had never been in an *americano* house. No one else was home. The kitchen was dazzling white and full of machinery.

They went up to Michael's room. He had his own bed; books, games, a train, even a radio. Jose sat on the edge of the bed, smiling and nodding, touching something now and then, yet not wanting to let the red-hair know he'd never seen a boy's room so full of things.

In late afternoon, he went back to Cabin 6 to tell Giron about it, the words rushing out. He told him everything except the fact that he now thought he'd like to have white skin and red hair like Miguel. Speak English and live in a house like that.

Sunday morning, Jose dressed for mass, putting on a fresh shirt and clean pants, getting his black boots out of tissue paper beneath the bunk. Giron had reluctantly agreed to take him in, and they locked Sanchez in the cabin.

On the way, Jose said, "I think I should go to confession soon."

"Certainly," Giron replied. "I'll have to check the priest's schedule."

"Should I tell the priest about the fence? Where I'm from?"

Giron looked over. "You don't need to go that far. No one has ever told a priest absolutely everything."

Jose laughed. That's what Enrique had said, too.

They didn't have to walk all the way. One of the flat-beds chugged past them and stopped. They brushed the field dirt off and leaped up to the rough boards.

MISSION SAN RAMON had been periodically rebuilt since the early 1900s and was constructed in the familiar square-fort form, a Moorish-style, bell-towered church dominating the southwest corner. Inside the square were the gardens, a patio, and a walkway, which were usually occupied by swarms of white pigeons. Some of the early friars and their Indian converts were buried in the gardens, spaced around the Fourteen Stations of the Cross.

On the other three sides of the square were the original workshops, storerooms, and kitchen. From the end of the church and sacristy, under thick, vine-wrapped arches, were the old padre and guest rooms. They now housed Father Lebeon, the mission priest, his brother monks, and his staff. Two storerooms had been converted into a museum, displaying ancient Bibles, books on medicine, Indian paintings, branding irons for the mission cattle, old vestments, and prayer books.

Jose and Giron strolled around until eleven and then went into the church. The padre was a compact, dark-haired man. His cheeks were pale, with a spot of color near each cheekbone.

Jose whispered to Giron, "He looks very tough."

Like his father, he had always been afraid of priests. They represented great authority.

Giron nodded.

After a while, Father Lebeon began delivering his sermon in English, which was of little satisfaction to Jose. He'd always been bored by sermons, anyway, even in Baja. He liked the ceremony, the music, the stained-glass windows, the statues, but never the sermons.

Yet this was a beautiful church, quite unlike any he'd ever seen. It was by far the oldest church he'd been in. It was not as fancy as the big one in Ensenada; not half the size, either. But there was something very peaceful about it.

When the mass was over, the noon Angelus was rung by one of the Franciscan brothers. As they went out into the bright sunshine, to the tolling of the bell, Jose asked, "What'll we do this afternoon?"

Looking down the length of San Ramon, which seemed abandoned, Giron sighed. There was really nothing to do. "If I was back in Los Angeles, I'd probably go sailing with a friend of mine off Long Beach. And I'd take you. But here . . . I think we'd better just go back to the camp and lie under the pepper trees. I've got some work to do on my notes."

Jose groaned.

But as they walked away, Giron said, "I hear we'll have a day off next week. Before we shift to picking cucumbers. You and I will go to Salinas, a city north of here. Not as large as Los Angeles or San Francisco but large enough. How's that?"

"Couldn't I be caught?"

Giron laughed. "No, put that out of your mind. You've seen all the Mexicans around here. You look no different from them."

That was true, Jose thought. He just felt different.

That afternoon, Jose took three hours to draw a portrait of Giron and then presented it to him.

"It's terrific, Jose," Giron said. "It looks just like me."

He did not say the ears were too big.

11

THE TOMATO FIELDS were finished Monday. They worked until dark to load the last lugs. There would be a later pick when more ripened. But now the loading platforms were jammed with boxes labeled "Bright-Pack." Heavy diesel trucks were being filled and lumbered out periodically. The pickers would not work again until Wednesday morning. Some of the men had already left Haines Main to go on to other farms. Not so many would be needed for the cucumbers.

Just past seven on Tuesday morning, Jose and Giron walked and hitched to San Ramon to catch the Greyhound north. Giron wore slacks, a yellow jumper, and expensive-looking shoes. Jose was proud to be with him. He looked more *americano* than Mexican.

As they sat down, far in the back, Jose whispered, "Did you see how the bus driver stared at me?"

Giron laughed it off. "Put it out of your mind." As he dug his shoulders into the soft seat, he added, "As a matter of fact, Mexico used to own this state. You and I are the new Mexican army. We'll take it back again."

Jose laughed, too, feeling less like a criminal.

The bus began to speed along the freeway, skirting the Salinas River. "That is part of the reason the earth is so good here, Jose. But it's a strange river. Sometimes it runs on the surface; sometimes underground for long distances."

"You know a lot of things," Jose said.

Giron smiled. "I know we will conquer Salinas."

Jose decided to pretend, just for the day, that Giron was his father. Giron was dressed so well, and was so confident about everything. Maldonado would not mind, he knew.

The countryside became even more fertile as they went north. In some fields, dozens of irrigation nozzles swished back and forth, sending great sprays of shining water across the crops. Back on the yellowed hills to the east, at the beginning of the mountains, cattle grazed. Jose wondered if Baja would ever look like this.

They rode in silence for a while and then Giron said, "We'll walk around, see the stores, have a good meal. Perhaps we can find a movie this afternoon."

Jose nodded happily. He'd been to the cinema once in Ensenada; the second trip there, when he was eleven.

"You should see Cantinflas. Maybe we can find a Cantinflas film. There are several Spanish movies in Salinas."

Jose had heard of Cantinflas and had seen posters of his films. He was a comedian with a face like an egg and a small mustache.

Giron turned in his seat. "I have an idea. When I was a student at Los Angeles State, we used to try to find everything that was free in town. It's a good game, I'll show you."

The bus ducked down off the freeway to stop for a few minutes in several small towns and then they were in Salinas.

Jose was awed by the city. Salinas made Ensenada appear as small as San Vicente. He couldn't imagine what Los Angeles might be like.

As they moved along the busy street, shops and stores crammed against each other, everyone hurrying somewhere, Jose noticed a secretive smile on Giron's face. Suddenly, the teacher nudged him. "In here," he said. They turned into a large store.

"It's like a department store, but it's really a pharmacy," Giron said, as they went through a turnstile.

He paused a moment, looking around. He had the air of the officials who sometimes drove down from Ensenada to inspect finished road work, Jose thought. They always held their noses up high.

There weren't many customers this early. The clerks

were busy stocking shelves and dusting them. Everything from candy and toys to canvas chairs and fishing rods was on sale. In the back of the store was a *farmacia* counter.

Stopping by one counter, Giron said, "Ah, hah, here we are." All sorts of razors, the straight kind, the safety kind, and the ones with motors on them, were being sold. In front of one variety was a sign: "Free Demonstration." Jose translated, *Demostracion Gratis.* Some words in English were very close to Spanish.

Giron cleared his throat importantly and picked up the electric razor. It whirred over his chin. Eyebrows raised, he studied the path of the razor in a small mirror on the counter. He was acting like a *Numero Uno,* a "Number One," customer.

"Will you buy it?"

"Not at all." Giron grinned.

When he had finished shaving, he placed the razor down thoughtfully, inspected his face, grunted approval, and said, "Come along, we have other things to do here."

At another counter there was a rack of small bottles with rubber bulbs on top. Giron looked them over and lifted one off. He said, "I am pretending I am Cantinflas." Pointing the bulb toward his face, he squeezed it.

Jose stifled a laugh. The clerk was only a few feet away. Perfume was heavy in the air. Giron shot a squirt toward Jose.

The clerk said, "Now, mister."

Giron replaced the bottle and bowed slightly.

On the way out, he said, "See, I told you how many things are free in this country." They left the drugstore, laughing as if they'd defeated the entire American Army.

"Now, we will attack a supermarket," Giron said.

They began searching for one, pausing once in front of an automobile place. The shining cars, doors invitingly open, stood on deep red carpets. Giron said, "If we were not just on holiday, we would go inside and I would say, 'I am Rafael Giron, a millionaire from Los Angeles, and I am thinking of buying a new car.' They would give us a Cadillac, of course, and we would drive round and round. Then we'd go back, and I'd say, 'I don't like this one, how about that one?'"

They found a Safeway and sampled a cheese dip. The next store wasn't so generous, but at a third one a lady in a pink apron was serving small cups of a new chocolate drink. Giron raved over it in Spanish until the woman's mouth dropped. They got a free yardstick in a hardware store and a free balloon in a shoe store. And each time they came out they burst into laughter.

Then Giron led Jose up and down several streets until they came to a small store that had a palette on the window. It was an art supply store. Easels and tubes of paint and wooden mannequins were on display.

Giron nodded. "Let's go in."

The store was crammed with canvasses, frames, tubes of paint, art books and things that Jose had never seen.

At the counter, Giron said, "All right, you're the expert. Tell me what you need to start painting. But be reasonable."

"I don't know, *señor*." Just looking around would have been enough. Jose found it hard to think.

Giron asked the woman at the counter and she began putting tubes in front of them. Giron held one up. "Grumbacher's Finest Zinc White. Is this all right?"

Jose nodded.

"And how about some Cadmium Yellow, Pale?"

Jose nodded again.

"And some Thalo Yellow, Green."

Jose said, "*Señor* Giron..."

Giron laughed. "Cadmium Red, Deep. I've never heard of these colors."

"Neither have I."

The saleswoman put four more out, along with two brushes and six small mounted canvasses.

"It is too much," Jose protested.

Giron shrugged and asked for the price.

"Eleven dollars and sixty cents," said the woman.

Giron looked down at Jose. "It's very expensive to be a painter," he said.

"Put them back," Jose said. It was too expensive.

Giron laughed. "Oh, what the hell." He paid the woman, and they went out again, Jose clutching the large bag, thanking Giron profusely.

On the street, Jose said, "I promise you that someday I'll be as famous as Orozco."

"You shoot high enough," Giron said, chuckling.

Finally, at about four o'clock, after they'd had lunch and seen a film, Giron said, "Now, I'll treat myself."

Jose stood outside a bar with dice on its windows and watched as the teacher went in and had two straight drinks. They went down bang, bang. He came out rubbing his belly and grinning.

They caught the 4:35 Greyhound to San Ramon. There had never been such a good day, Jose thought. *Los Estados Unidos* was everything he'd dreamed of.

12

NOT LONG AFTER they'd returned to Haines Main, the man from next door, Cubria, the checker player, knocked on the cabin and asked Giron if he'd like to go into Paso Robles; have a few beers, maybe look at the girls.

"You mind?" Giron asked.

Jose was sitting on the bed, looking at the tubes of paint, feeling the bristles of the brushes, and running his fingers over the canvasses. "No. I'll take Sanchez for a walk. I'll be all right."

Giron left just before dark. Jose took the dog behind the rows of cabins and out into the fields. He felt sorry for him. The one bad thing about having Sanchez along was penning him up each day. In Colnett, he'd roamed at will; sometimes trotting all the way to the village to pry into the garbage can by the Garcia store.

Sanchez snooped over the fields, running and stopping; sniffing, then running on; looking back now and then to make certain Jose was following.

It was just after nine when Jose and Sanchez got back to Haines Main. The lights were on in the barracks and some of the cabins, but there weren't many men around.

As they passed by the barracks, Jose heard a voice he knew he had heard before.

A figure moved out of the shadow of the barracks, blocking his way. It was the man from the shower. A slice of light from the barracks window illuminated his face. He was grinning and he smelled of wine. He was not wearing his false teeth.

"I think you're gonna be friendly to me, boy. That black man's gone to another farm, and your roomie's out, too. Now, you shouldn't of thrown that soap in my face. I was jus' tryin' to be nice."

Jose did not understand the words, but he was frightened at the soft tone. "No, *señor*," he said.

"Let's jus' you and I sit down here, an' talk a while."

"*Por favor, señor.*" Jose hoped someone would come out of the barracks. He could hear voices and a radio playing in there.

"Take it easy, boy," the man said, grabbing for his wrist.

Jose tugged back, repeating, "*Por favor, señor.*"

There was a snarl by his ear, and Sanchez's wide jaws clamped on the man's arm. Jose fell back. He rolled over and saw Sanchez tearing at the arm. The *americano* was screaming.

On his feet, Jose grabbed the dog by his ears and wrenched him back. Sanchez was still snarling. His teeth were bared, and there was blood on them.

The *americano* was wallowing back and forth on the ground, clutching his arm, yelling. Men poured out of the barracks.

Jose stood holding Sanchez, dazed and shaken.

Kneeling down, one of the *pochos* said in Spanish, "We better get him to a hospital." He turned to Jose. "That dog do this?"

"It was an accident, *señor*."

An *americano* worker said, "Somebody get Eddie. Tell him to bring a gun."

Jose understood "Eddie" and "gun," and said, "No, *señor. Por favor*." He began backing up.

The *americano* said, "I'll get the dog."

As he advanced, Sanchez snarled again, showing his teeth, straining to get loose.

The *pocho* yelled, "Watch him. He's a killer."

Jose wheeled and began running toward Cabin 6, looking back once, Sanchez at his heels.

Inside the cabin, Jose pulled the mattress away and jammed the Colnett money into his pocket. He was stuffing some of his clothes into the suitcase when he heard shouts from up near the barracks and the sound of a car starting.

Sanchez stood by the door, his back hairs up and bristling. Jose said to him, "We must go. They will shoot you."

Putting the art supplies in, he slammed the suitcase shut and left the cabin. "Hurry," he said to Sanchez, but the dog was already plunging ahead.

They went behind the cabin and started across the fields toward the railroad tracks, Jose running as fast as he could with the half-packed suitcase.

They were gone before Eddie arrived at No. 6, carrying a 30.30.

Book II

THE MIRACLE

1

SAN RAMON WAS DECAYING. Until the freeway had cut it off two years previously, bypassed it with a sweeping curve, it had been a lively little town on the royal road, El Camino Real, historic old No. 101. Now, much of it was abandoned and boarded up. Some of the doorways were littered.

There were exactly seven square blocks to the business district—two blocks on the east side of the Real, five on the west. Once, truckers had stopped at Olcott's Service Station to gurgle down gallons of diesel fuel or gasoline. People had come from Atascadero and Cholame and San Ardo to buy groceries at Estaban Cole's market, tools at San Ramon Hardware, and furniture from Nello Solari; or to have beef stew at the Dinner Bell, or a beer at Pook Goodwin's Mission Bell Bar.

Now, they found it simpler to roll out on the banked lanes and go south to San Luis Obispo or north to King

City. The drugstore had been abandoned. So had the dry goods store across from the mission and seven other shops. Their windows were either boarded or grimy.

Once, the town could depend on at least three hundred visitors a day to Mission San Ramon, which stood about forty feet off El Camino Real. In addition to dropping silver in the poor box and spending perhaps a dollar at the mission store, the visitors were usually good for at least five dollars in meals and gas in the town itself.

Now, the only mission visitors seemed to be the buffs. Even the busloads of schoolchildren from nearby communities, herded together for a historical outing, had ceased to come. An exceptional day could tally no more than twenty-five visitors. On some days, when the winter mist lay cold over the Salinas Valley, Father Lebeon would pray for even five visitors, and the sandaled, brown-robed Franciscan brothers, their *capuchos* pulled up over their heads, would have been willing to settle for three.

As much as anything, the village of San Ramon had lost its will to survive.

On most nights, Frank Olcott kept his filling station open until one, simply in hopes of capturing an extra dollar for the day. Sometimes, farmers gassed their pickups around eleven after a few drinks at Pook's. Olcott, who was sixty-three years old, seldom slept well anyway because of an old back injury. He kept a pot of coffee on for any eye-weary traveler going slow enough to take the San Ramon off-ramp.

In addition to owning the station, Olcott had been mayor of San Ramon for over twenty years, as well as its only peace officer. In this capacity, he had little to do. He always wore his badge, but sometimes it made him feel silly. The only disturbance amounting to anything usually occurred Saturday nights at the Mission Bell. He'd hobble down the Real, stick his head in the door of Pook's place and yell, "Anyone want to fight a cripple?" That usually did it.

Tall, balding, a stoop-shouldered man with a farmer's ruddy face and sharp gray eyes, Olcott had been struggling to save San Ramon ever since the freeway dried it up. He'd formed a committee to publicize Mission San Ramon, but no one had any suggestions for persuading motorists to slow down to twenty-five and take the exit. He'd even requested the government to declare San Ramon a distressed area. Nothing had worked.

In the past year, there had been moments when he was ready to join his fellow townsmen in a mass evacuation. But then he'd take a walk around the seven failing blocks and decide not to leave. It was the only town he'd ever known.

A few minutes after one, Olcott saw headlights coming toward him and recognized Father Lebeon's dusty half-ton truck from the mission, hay bales stacked in the back.

In the lot next door, Jose Maldonado Alvarez pulled Sanchez deeper into the shadows by a pile of broken machinery crates. He was waiting for the station to close so that he could get water. The headlights had startled him.

Four hundred feet away, Olcott said, "You're up a little late, Father Lebeon."

The powerfully built priest slid out of the cab and yawned. "People who need last rites don't pick the time." Although clean-shaven, his beard was so blue-black that by last morning mass he appeared grizzly. This time of night, he always had a stubble.

Born in Marseilles, a French seaport, Lebeon tended to be a practical priest rather than one concerned with holy niceties. He'd been assigned to San Ramon after serving the Indians at Mescalaro, New Mexico, and he spoke fluent Spanish as well as French and English. Much to the amusement of the seven Franciscan brothers at the mission, Lebeon had constructed a chinning bar in the barn, and for a time before his fortieth birthday had punched a heavy bag to take out frustrations. His chief regret was that he had not lived in 1794, when the mission was founded. He preferred a rough life.

"I didn't think you'd be open, Frank," he said. "I need a quart of oil for the tractor. Brother Carlos made me promise I'd get it."

"Shouldn't be open, Padre." Olcott went to the oil rack. "Haven't had a paying customer since ten o'clock."

Jose watched them in the dim lights by the pumps. He could hear the murmur of English and for a moment thought about going up and asking the priest for help. But even at this distance, he looked so tough. There was no telling what he might do. It was better to hide and wait for his father.

"Maybe I'm your last sale for tonight," Lebeon said, looking up the deserted highway.

More and more, this village reminded him of the Latin wording on the sundial of that mission in San Gabriel: *Horae omnes vulnerant ultima necat.* It meant, "Every hour wounds, the last one kills." The hours were ticking off.

Olcott snorted. "That damnable freeway." It was odd how they always got back to the same subject. He glanced off toward the wide white paths of concrete that swept by the village, speared now and then by car or truck lights.

"It's progress, Frank."

"Wish you'd talk turkey with God to slow it down," Olcott replied sourly.

Lebeon smiled. "Put the oil on the bill, will you?"

"Why not? I do it for everyone else."

The priest climbed back into the truck. The engine turned over, and the pickup crunched over the gravel apron, as Olcott began padlocking the pumps.

A car coming from the other direction caught Jose in a circle of strong light, and he jumped behind the pile of packing cases, losing his footing and falling backward. He yelled as a long splinter pierced his thin jacket and entered the flesh of his left shoulder.

Olcott heard the yelp and turned, peering toward the vacant lot.

The pain was fierce. Jose reached up to his shoulder and found that the spike of wood had driven through. He realized that he was impaled on the packing-case slat. He tried to lift himself with his right hand but almost passed out. One end of the board was still attached to the case, on an angle to the earth.

There was nothing to do but call for help. He took a deep breath. *"Ayuda! Ayuda!"* he shouted. Sanchez, standing protectively over him, began to bark loudly.

Olcott got his flashlight and headed in the direction of the barking, wondering what kind of nonsense was going on next door. The beam of his flashlight finally picked up the boy and dog by the splintered crating, left over from better days when he had sold irrigation pumps.

Shining the light into the small, stricken face, Olcott asked, "Now, what are you doin' out here this time o' night, and how the devil did you do that?"

"Ayuda," Jose said weakly but sucked in his breath when he spotted the badge on the man's chest.

Sanchez kept on barking, his tail whipping. He was still straddling Jose.

"Get that dumb dog away, and I'll help you," Olcott said gruffly.

Jose spoke to Sanchez in Spanish, calming him down. The mongrel moved aside but eyed Olcott, making low noises in his throat.

Olcott came over and knelt. "Good Lord, you did it up brown. That went right through." He pulled the jacket and shirt aside. "There's a half inch stickin' out. Sharp as a nail."

Jose closed his eyes so as not to see the badge.

"All right now, just lay still, and I'll get a hand under you. We'll go straight up. This is gonna hurt, boy."

The words were meaningless, but Jose gritted his teeth as Olcott's fingers worked under his shoulder. He refused to cry, but a groan came out.

"Here we go, up."

There was a red flash of pain, and then it was over and Olcott had pulled the shoulder free. Jose felt himself being lifted to his feet. His knees were wobbly.

"All right, boy, I'll take you to Doc Atherton's and wake him up. But somebody ought to pound your behind for being out so late." Then Olcott spotted the suitcase. "What you doin'? Runnin' away?"

Jose took several steadying breaths. He was certain this man would turn him over to *la migra,* then go looking for his father.

He moved back a couple of steps, scooped up the suitcase, and darted off toward El Camino Real. Olcott shouted, "Hey, come back here, boy."

But Jose and Sanchez were already out of sight, and Olcott hadn't run ten feet in twenty years.

He muttered, "I'll be double damned," and shook his head. "Crazy Mex kid." He went back to the service station and turned off all lights except the one over the cash register.

JOSE MADE IT several hundred yards along the Real and then stopped. The shoulder hurt, but it was his stomach that was giving him the most trouble. He felt queasy. He looked back toward the station. The stoop-shouldered man with the badge wasn't following. He went on.

When they were almost opposite the mission, he said to Sanchez, "I must rest. We'll hide until morning."

They went up the worn, uneven adobe steps and into the nave. It was dimly lighted by a bank of prayer candles near the confessional booth and the wooden statue of Christ. There were more candles near the railing before the tabernacle at the front of the church. Jose crossed himself and looked around, feeling safer already.

But he was worried about someone coming in. He glanced up at the choir loft and started for the steep steps, Sanchez trotting behind.

They reached the top, and the hand-hewn floorboards creaked as they moved to the far side. Jose lowered himself down, sprawling against the cold outer wall, his left shoulder extending over the last board, which was spaced about six inches from the plaster-covered adobe. Letting out a long, shuddering breath, he said weakly, "I'm sure I'll be all right in an hour or so, Sanchez." His voice sounded hollow in the empty church.

The dog lay down, massive head between his paws.

There were twenty or so chairs at the front of the loft, near the solid wooden balcony railing. An old foot-pumped organ stood behind them. Nothing else was up there. Suddenly, Jose longed for the safety of Colnett. He could picture Enrique out there in the lee of the cape, pulling the anchor up, ready to move on to another spot. The pelicans would be beating north; maybe some gulls working a school of anchovies.

With dull eyes, he stared off through the darkness to the Immaculate Conception over the tabernacle. There were wooden statues of the saints in the ornate *retablo,* the decorated framework. A flickering sanctuary lamp, hung on a chain from the ceiling to the left of the altar, casting a peaceful glow on it. He prayed soundlessly to the Virgin Mary to help him. In a few moments, he dozed off.

Blood, seeping slowly through his jacket and shirt from the small puncture, dropped down through the wide crack in the flooring. It splattered the ancient Indian-crafted statue of Christ on the Cross, which stood in the nave on a simple wooden box about twenty-five feet inside the church directly below the loft and against the left wall.

Drops rolled slowly down the gold-inscribed I.N.R.I., which was on the top of the cross. The letters stood for: "Jesus of Nazareth, King of The Jews." A thin rivulet landed on the shoulder; then ebbed slowly down His chest.

In a few minutes, with Jose resting quietly, the wound stopped bleeding.

2

THREE HOURS LATER, the light that had begun spreading softly down over the Gabilan Mountains to the east was chalky and pale gray. Josefa Espinosa, a woman of sixty-four, dressed entirely in black and wearing crumbling shoes, stalked down the middle of the Real. She was built like a stubby water tank.

At one point she mumbled to herself, *"Manolo me esta agotando la paciencia."* She continually lost patience with Manuel, her husband. Mainly, she was annoyed because he wouldn't walk the four miles to the mission with her each morning.

Josefa worked as a housekeeper for a Swiss-American family near San Ardo and took the first bus there each day after devotions. She had long ago given up hope that Manuel would provide luxury, but she had faith someday something would happen to lift the Espinosas to a life of ease.

She did a flanking left turn at the church steps. The door banged shut, and her heavy footsteps thudded down the aisle. Her head was covered with a thin, black shawl. She looked neither left nor right as she bore down on the altar.

Jose awakened at the noise, but it took a few seconds for him to realize where he was. He saw that Sanchez was already up—alert, and looking down. Sitting up, he felt stiff, and his shoulder throbbed.

He held his hand toward Sanchez to keep him quiet and crossed the loft in a crouch, hunkering down to peer over the solid wooden railing. He saw the old woman and heard her prayer, which was being delivered in little less than a shout, rapid-fire. More or less, it was the same request of years.

"...*un buen esposo para mi hija Dorotea...una casa chica para Manolo y mi...una pequeña pensión para dos ancianos que lo merecen...*"

Jose got most of it: "I am not a selfish woman, so only ask for a good husband for my daughter Dorothy...a small house for Manuel and me...a small pension for two old and worthy people..."

Finally, Josefa strained herself up, made the sign of the cross over her great bosom, and began to pad back down the aisle toward the church entrance.

Jose moved with her retreating footsteps, wanting to make sure she'd left the church. A floorboard creaked, and he stopped, almost at the top of the stairs.

Down below, the statue of Christ on the Cross had caught Josefa's eye. There was something different about it in the soft candle shine this morning. Reaching for her gold-rimmed glasses, she put them on her nose and stared at the statue. Both wonder and alarm passed over her face. She breathed out, "Mother of God. Oh, Mary, Mother of God."

Mouth open, she backed across the nave until her heavy buttocks were squarely against the confessional booth, and there was no more room to move. She stayed against it, murmuring, "Oh, oh..."

Jose heard the faint sounds and frowned down at the timbered floor, wondering what she was doing. Then he heard the front door burst open. Her yell of *"Milagro"* cut through the dawn like an axe.

He stared down. "Miracle?" Had the old woman lost her mind? He stayed poised at the head of the steps a moment longer, then whispered to Sanchez, "Come on." He crossed the loft, grabbed his suitcase, and left the church, skirting around Josefa's sprawled body on the adobe stoop. Overcome, she had prostrated herself and was praying.

Jose ran directly across the street, pausing in front of the abandoned dry goods store. "We must hide, Sanchez," he said. He looked in both directions, and then his eyes came back to the storefront with its grimy windows and boards. "There!"

They went around the side and up to the back door. Jose tried it. One hinge was almost off, but it creaked open. He peered inside. It was dingy and dust-covered; empty boxes were scattered around. Sanchez, sniffing, followed him in, and he closed the door.

3

FATHER LEBEON was preparing for the early devotions when he heard the commotion. He was in the sacristy, the little room in which the vestments and sacred communion vessels were kept, dressing for the six-thirty mass. He had just finished putting on the alb, the long, white linen garment that covered his robe.

He ran into the gardens and looked around in the thin light. Seeing no one, he went on through the iron gate to El Camino Real. He thought there might have been an accident. As he moved toward the church steps, he saw the sprawled figure. Going to her, he lifted the black shawl.

"Josefa," he said, in surprise. "What's wrong? Are you injured? Did you fall?" Gently, he pulled her into a sitting position.

She mumbled, "Mary, Mother of God," over and over.

Lebeon shook her. "Josefa, Josefa," he said, sharply. "Stop that!"

"*Milagro*," she moaned. "*Milagro*."

The priest sighed and sat down beside her on the damp steps. He put his arm around her huge, soft shoulder. It was really much too early for this, he thought. But he said, tenderly, shifting to Spanish, "Josefa, miracles happen every day. Mostly, we don't see them. Now, you'd better get your bus to San Ardo or you'll miss work. And I must finish dressing for mass." He glanced at the eastern horizon. It was barely yellow.

Josefa raised her head slowly and stared at him in disbelief. "A miracle! Inside!"

Lebeon nodded. "All miracles are inside there."

"Padre," she pleaded. "A miracle inside."

"All right, Josefa, where inside?"

"On His blessed body," she said, eyes glazed with excitement.

Lebeon looked at her a moment longer, then said, wearily, "All right, Josefa, show me."

"No! No! It is on His body. He bled for us."

Lebeon forced himself to be patient. It always seemed to be the very young or the very old who saw "miracles." "Stay here, Josefa," he said, rising from the steps.

He went inside, crossed himself, and then walked to the statue, his mouth opening suddenly, his forehead bunching in a frown. The stains, whatever they were, hadn't been there the previous evening. Father Lebeon usually spent a final moment of the day there.

He moved closer. It had come from above, that was

certain. He examined but did not touch the dried stain on I.N.R.I. Yes, it could be blood, he thought. It was reddish-brown. But so were a thousand other liquids. He lighted another prayer candle, and in its flickering glow traced the flow of the stain from I.N.R.I. down to His shoulder and then to His chest.

Certain that there was a simple and quite scientific explanation for it, Lebeon muttered, "Forgive me," and with a square fingernail scraped a fragment of the dried stain off the shoulder. He sniffed it, hoping that it would smell of paint or turpentine, but the timbers of the mission had seasoned almost two centuries before. No paint had touched its inner surfaces since the Indian converts had mashed wild flowers in the late 1700s to gain color for designs where the beams sank into the stone and adobe and on the rounded surface of the ceiling. He sniffed again. There was no odor.

Lebeon looked up, examining the area where the choir loft was braced over the nave. He knew there was a six-inch separation between the wall of the mission, which was four feet thick, and the first floorboard of the choir loft. He'd never been able to understand why the original friars had left that opening, but there it was, nonetheless.

Staring up at it, a slow smile crossed his face. *That was the answer!* Gonzalvo, the mission handyman, had probably kicked over a can of colored detergent or some kind of cleaning fluid. He ran to the steps, cupping a hand over the candle to keep the flame from blowing out. It occurred to him that he should turn on the lights, but the switch was in the sacristy, and it would take too much time. He'd turn them on when he brought the brothers in to see a "miracle that wasn't a miracle."

He got down on his hands and knees and searched the wide timbers for signs of cleaning fluid or any other kind of liquid. There were none. Neither was there any indication of someone having been up there during the night. He let out a slow whistle, sitting back on his haunches.

A few minutes later, he descended the steps slowly and sat down in the last pew, crossing his arms. Now and then he glanced up at the loft or over to the statue. Finally, he gave up. He would bring the brothers in and awaken Gonzalvo, who had probably been the last person in the loft. He arose, genuflected, and went out. He would have to hurry. Mass was only fifteen minutes away.

He'd forgotten entirely about Josefa Espinosa, and on reaching the steps found that she was gone. He let out a breath. All he needed was Josefa shrieking *"Milagro"* all over the valley before he had a chance to explain what had happened, and, perhaps, why.

He looked down the Real. Maisie Keeper was at the door of the Dinner Bell, opening up.

Sam Ramon was beginning to stir.

4

JOSE HAD EXPLORED the store. The counters and shelves were still in place. There was a lot of trash on the floor. Air came through the part of the front window that was smashed and boarded up. The rest of the window was still good but was so covered with dust that he could barely see out. The front door was also boarded.

In the back of the room empty wine bottles, old milk containers, empty cans, and bread wrappers were strewn around. Perhaps *vagabundos*, tramps, had spent a night or two there.

He sat down on a pile of carpet matting, trying to figure out what to do. Sanchez came over close and plopped down. Jose stroked the thick, coarse hairs on his back.

He knew that he should get some medicine for his shoulder. It did not seem any worse, but the ache was still there and it hurt when he moved his left arm. His father had warned him about taking care of cuts.

He'd opened his shirt and looked at the wound. It was a tiny hole, but already there was a circle of red around it. The back of his shoulder ached.

He wanted to let Giron know where he was so that when Maldonado finally got to Haines Main, they could find each other. He was also getting very hungry.

Finally, he decided to change the stained jacket and shirt, get something to eat, and feed Sanchez. Then he would walk out to the fields and locate Giron.

It was painful to slip out of the clothing, but he did it slowly and carefully, wincing as he put on a new shirt and tucked it in.

He considered taking Sanchez with him but decided not to. Someone from Haines might see them.

The dog trotted over to the door with him, and whined briefly as he closed it again. He slipped past the high weeds around the back door and out to the alleyway behind the row of stores, moving along it the whole block before turning out onto El Camino Real. The few people he saw were going into the mission for early mass. The old woman wasn't around; there was no one at the gas station.

He walked rapidly to the Dinner Bell and went in. There were two customers on the stools, both *americanos* and not from Haines Main.

Maisie Keeper, the bantam, dyed-blond wife of Neil Keeper, owner of the Bell, was behind the counter. Maisie smiled at Jose. "What'll it be, young man?"

Jose pointed at a round plastic case.

"Doughnuts, huh?"

"*Si.*" He held up four fingers.

"Four."

"*Si.*"

"Anything else?"

"*Leche, por favor.*"

"Milk?"

"*Si, señora.*"

"To go?"

Jose frowned.

"In a carton like this?" She held up a pint.

"*Si, señora. Dos.*"

"Okay, two milks to go."

Jose nodded.

"There you are."

"*Muchas gracias.*"

She smiled. "You're welcome."

He gave her a dollar and got the change.

She watched him go, saying to one of the customers, "Cute kid, huh?"

JOSEFA HURRIED INTO the Espinosa house and practically fell over Manuel, who was groping around in his underwear for the coffee jar. Manuel, a small, birdlike man, was both frightened and pleased to see his wife. He was pleased because he couldn't find the coffee jar and frightened because something awful must have happened to send her back home again.

"Miracle," Josefa puffed.

Manuel examined her red face, which looked as though it were about to explode. "They gave you a raise and a day off."

Josefa swallowed and tried to catch her breath. She shook her head. "In the church. A miracle. I saw it."

Manuel shrugged and asked thickly, "What did you do with the coffee?"

"I saw blood on His body. On the statue."

"There is always blood on His body. It is on His hands and His feet and where the thorns . . ."

"There is new blood, Manolo," Josefa said. "Blood He sent. A sign for us all."

Manuel shook his head. "Josefa, you've missed your bus." He went to work at his own job in the dairy co-op at noon each day.

But Josefa had already gone. Through the windows he glimpsed her ponderously trotting over to their neighbors, the Panaderos.

5

SEVERAL HOURS LATER, Father Lebeon and Brothers Amos, Luke, Timothy, Noel, Anthony, Carlos, and Kevin were in the choir loft, studying absolutely nothing. They had been there for thirty minutes.

Lebeon had brought a flashlight up and had ordered Gonzalvo, a hulking, silent Chicano, who had been on the mission staff for eighteen years, to rig a stand-light for illumination directly above the statue. So far, there was no indication of any fluids up there; no evidence that anyone had been in the loft during the night. They'd found some dog hairs, but Gonzalvo's hound roamed all over the mission. He'd even been caught sleeping in the pews.

Lebeon and the brothers were mystified, and although they did not commit themselves beyond stating the belief that a "miracle" was always possible, they had examined the area with growing uneasiness. Even if

Josefa hadn't found the stain and spread the word, the incident would have been puzzling and unnerving.

Sharply questioned by Father Lebeon, Gonzalvo had sworn that he hadn't been in the loft since Friday and even then had taken no liquids of any kind up the steps. He'd simply swept it out and dusted the organ and the chairs. Yes, Mojo had been up there with him but was that a crime? He resented their accusing looks.

One by one, shaking their heads or shrugging, all the brothers except Amos, who was by far the oldest, left to go about their chores. In their excitement, they'd hurried the morning devotions, and Father Lebeon had transferred the early masses to the chapel, which he now realized was a mistake. It only helped the rumor sweep across the valley.

Lines of worry crisscrossing his face, he asked Brother Amos, "What do you think?"

Amos dug his sandaled toe around the timber of the loft and replied, "It isn't up to us to think, Father. If it is a miracle, we accept it gratefully."

Lebeon stared with annoyance at the round, soft monk's face. Senile old goat, he thought, and then regretted it. Amos had his *capuche* down, and the sparse white hair on his pink head stood straight up.

Lebeon said, "That is undoubtedly the most unsatisfactory answer I've ever heard from anyone on any topic. I didn't ask your acceptance, Amos. I asked your opinion."

"There being no visible sign of a reason up here, my opinion is that..."

"Careful," Lebeon warned.

But careful was Amos's middle name. "...is that it could be a miracle."

"That's the second most unsatisfactory answer I've ever heard," Father Lebeon said. "I'm surprised at you."

Brother Amos smiled. "I'm surprised at myself," he said softly. "But I'm not a father, or a bishop or a cardinal. And I'm not the Pope, you may be assured. Where miracles are concerned, I'd just as soon keep my opinion to myself. But you forced me."

Lebeon couldn't help laughing. "Now, that's an answer."

They snapped off the stand-light and went below to look at the statue again. After a moment of silence, Father Lebeon said, "I can't tell you why, but I don't think this is a miracle, I think it has some logical explanation. Wood simply does not bleed. It has sap, but it doesn't bleed."

"Unless?"

Lebeon threw up his hands. He simply didn't believe in miracles, although he'd never admitted it.

Amos said, "Well, you can do that, but do you know anybody with enough courage to spill anything on this statue?"

"Lebeon sighed. "No, I don't."

They looked at the statue a moment longer, and

Lebeon shook his head. "I'd like to know what logical explanation I can make to the newspaper reporters who are bound to come and to the bishop and parish. I haven't the faintest idea what to say."

"Why don't you just say you don't know?" Brother Amos replied.

The priest glanced at him skeptically.

They left the church, Amos exiting through the inner door to the sacristy at the rear. Father Lebeon took a bracing breath and went out the main door.

Several hundred feet away, near the parking area, he saw Josefa Espinosa fanning herself. She had already changed into her best dress and sat, queenlike, in a gaudy overstuffed chair. Lebeon faintly remembered having seen that chair in Solari's furniture store.

Manuel stood beside her, scrubbed up in the only complete suit he owned. He looked bewildered.

Around the steps were no less than fifty parishioners, many of whom had come to early mass and stayed on. They were all talking at once. Father Lebeon held up his hand for quiet.

"Yes, something has occurred in our church, but it is too early to call it a miracle. This morning *Señora* Josefa Espinosa discovered a stain on the statue of Christ."

One mass attendant spoke up. "But they said it was blood, not a stain."

Lebeon corrected her carefully. "It is the same color, Mrs. Sheehy."

An elderly man standing at the top of the steps added, "Gonzalvo said it was on His shoulder and chest..."

Mrs. Sheehy pressed anxiously, "Is it a miracle?"

Father Lebeon skipped over her question to answer the elderly man. "Gonzalvo is right. Whatever it is, it is on His shoulder and chest."

"Is it a miracle?" Mrs. Sheehy demanded.

Father Lebeon looked at her with exasperation.

"I don't know. We will have experts study it. We'll test the stain, and the bishop will undoubtedly assign a commission within a few days to investigate."

A teenager, books in hand, asked, "But wouldn't that be sacrilegious, Father? In case the wood did bleed? To doubt it, Father?"

He gave her a perplexed look. "No, it would not be sacrilegious to make such a test. Now, run on to school or Mother Regina will skin you."

Then he addressed them all. "This is your church. I think you should see for yourselves, and make your individual decisions. Please come inside."

He stood away from the door as they mounted the steps, some of them looking as if they were about to journey over the horizon. He was afraid of veneration—the worship of the miracle itself. Once, in France, he'd seen a procession begin with breathtaking speed at the mere mention of a miracle. Nowadays, people were grasping at anything. And San Ramon was in a mood to dig for the rainbow's end.

As the last parishioner entered, and Father Lebeon was going down the steps, Frank Olcott labored up. "Mornin', Padre."

Lebeon, occupied with thoughts of the press and their questions, glanced up absentmindedly. "Oh, good morning, Frank."

"Hear we've got a little excitement. Maisie Keeper called me at home."

"That we have. But don't ask me how or why. All we found up there was some dog hair."

"If it's okay, I'll go in and look."

Lebeon said, "Your church as well as mine, Frank." Then he went on to his small, book-jammed office.

6

FEELING THE KNIFE-EDGED probing in his back as he climbed the final step (stairs always seemed to grind at his backbone), Olcott went in to look at the stain, staying at the rear of the crowd that was already pressing close to the statue. Gonzalvo had roped it off so that it wouldn't be within arm's length. There were subdued *ohs* and *ahs*, and Olcott heard the murmur of prayer.

He looked first at the stains and then up at the choir loft, studying the six-inch space between the mission wall and the first floorboard. Like Father Lebeon, Olcott had never quite believed in miracles.

Dog hair, he thought. It didn't make sense.

As he was leaving the church he heard a man whispering, "People will be comin' for miles around to see this."

He eased himself down the steps and limped the two blocks back to his station, a vague notion bothering him.

He unlocked the door and went over to the counter, plugging in the coffee pot.

A car pulled up to the gas pump area, and he went outside. He was so preoccupied that he overfilled the tank and apologized profusely as he wiped off the bumper.

The car drove out, and Olcott stood by the pumps, gazing off toward the piles of crating in the empty lot. Maybe, just maybe, he thought.

He limped over and stood by them, finally kicking the board that had snared the Mex kid. That dog had been a monster, he remembered, and the kid had run off into the Real, sure scared of something. Maybe he'd gone into the mission.

Olcott looked up there. It was as good a guess as any. Some miracle.

As he started back toward the mission, he thought again about the man saying, "People will be comin' for miles around."

Frowning slightly, he stopped. He was positive he'd never seen that kid before, and like as not, he was a runaway. He might be as far north as Salinas by now. Anyway, the boy spoke no English and wasn't likely to butt in

Finally, Olcott made up his mind. He was grinning as he went on back to the station.

IT WAS ABOUT eleven when Jose located the cucumber fields a kilometer south of the Haines tomato acreage. He stood on the road for a few minutes, making certain that neither Eddie nor Klosterman was around. He could see Rafael Giron stooping over the mounds of vines, along with about twelve other pickers. They were filling hampers. He walked on into the field and called to Giron.

"Jose, I was worried about you. They told me what happened, and I drove Cubria's car all over town looking for you."

"I'm sorry Sanchez caused trouble. Is that man all right?"

"Who cares?" said Giron. "I heard about him."

Several of the pickers were looking at them but soon bent to work again. The field foreman didn't seem to be around.

"Where's the dog?"

"In San Ramon. I found a place to hide. In that old store across from the mission."

"You're better off. I talked to Eddie this morning. Your father can find another place to work, but I'll try to collect your money."

Jose nodded. He didn't want to go back to Haines Main, anyway.

Giron stepped closer. "Is something wrong? You look pale."

"Yes, *señor,* I fell last night and hurt my shoulder."

"How did you do that?"

"A car came by, and I slipped and fell backwards. A long splinter drove into it."

"Ouch," said Giron. "Let me see."

Jose unbuttoned his shirt, and peeled it away at the top. "It aches," he said.

"I guess it does. It's swollen, too. Come over to the truck. There's a first aid kit in it, I think."

They went over to the flat-bed cab, and Giron found the kit. "You should go to a hospital. A puncture wound can be dangerous."

"No hospital," said Jose. "Please."

"Why not?" Giron pulled out a small bottle of alcohol.

"People go there to die."

Giron laughed. "Not always, Jose. But I'll get you to a doctor. You should have a shot."

Jose made an effort to remain still as Giron cleaned both sides of the wound with cotton dipped in alcohol. "I don't know what else to put on it," he said. He found some Band-Aids and stripped the paper from them, placing them back and front. Spilling some aspirin into his hand, he said, "Take two of these now and two more in four hours." He chuckled. "I sound like a doctor."

Jose felt better just being able to talk to Giron. "I'll be all right," he said.

"I'm sure you will. But go back there and lie down. I'll borrow Cubria's car again tonight, and we'll find a doctor. Okay?"

"Okay. But I wish my father would come."

"So do I," said Giron. I'll tell the office to let me know when he arrives."

"*Señor* Eddie?"

"Who else?"

"Then he'll find me and shoot Sanchez."

Giron shook his head. "No, he won't. I'll make certain he doesn't. Now, go on back to town and stay in that store. Keep off your feet."

Jose went back out to the road, staying well off to one side in case Eddie happened along. He skirted the freeway for the last kilometer.

THERE WAS A CROWD outside the mission, and he saw the old woman who had been in the church that morning sitting on a large chair near the parking lot. A small group of people were around her. He could not read the red-lettered sign by her chair, which said: "Courtesy—Solari's Furniture Store."

Jose finally worked up the courage to go to the edge of the crowd and tap a spectator on the shoulder. In his straw hat and jeans, he looked like a field worker. "What happened?" he asked.

"She saw a miracle."

Jose frowned. "What kind of miracle?"

"The statue of Christ bled."

She had cried out, *"Milagro,"* Jose remembered. He'd heard about miracles before but very little. A famous one had happened in Mexico, his mother had told him. "That's lucky," he said.

The picker shrugged and laughed.

Jose decided he would come back and see it when he felt better. He was a little dizzy from the long walk, and he was hungry again. He went on to Esteban Cole's, bought some crackers, sandwich meat, a can of dog food for Sanchez, and some milk.

Sanchez greeted him wildly, hopping up and down, tail thrashing. Jose opened the can of dog food with the horn-handled knife, fed Sanchez, and then ate the crackers and sandwich meat.

Before going to sleep on the matting, he went out to the front of the store and peered through the grime. The old lady was still there, and the crowd seemed to be growing larger. A taco vendor had rolled his pushcart up near her chair and was doing a good business.

He had not thought a miracle would be quite like this.

7

IN THE EARLY EVENING, Father Lebeon entered the nave and spent almost an hour staring at the statue, wondering if he should close the mission to all visitors until he'd received definite instructions. That, at least, might dampen the enthusiasm in San Ramon. His head had been throbbing dully since after lunch. Finally, he turned, feeling the presence of someone in the nave.

It was a middle-aged man dressed in a loud sports coat with a tie that appeared to have come out of a paint pot. He had a sketch pad.

After a moment Lebeon rose, asking politely, "May I help you?"

"Don't believe so," the visitor replied, busily sketching.

Father Lebeon glanced over the man's shoulder at the pad. The likeness of Christ was there, rendered with fair accuracy. But it was the marginal notes that upset the priest.

One said, "Blood on the signpost, I.N.R.I., whatever that means." Another said, "Splotch shaped like a pear on the shoulder; drip marks on chest."

"May I ask what you're doing?"

"Just getting it right, Reverend," the man replied.

"For what purpose?"

The man turned. "Miniatures, of course." He passed a card to Lebeon. "We can make 'em up in plastic for a dime, sell 'em here for fifty cents. Stock every store in town."

The card said: Bay Novelty Company, Burlingame. Lebeon reached across and crumpled the sketch pad.

"Please leave," he said, tiredness in his voice rather than anger.

"Hey, what's wrong with you?"

"Leave," Lebeon repeated.

The man got belligerent. "This is a church, ain't it? Public place? I'm in a legal, commercial business, Reverend. So what's your problem? You want a cut?"

Lebeon said quietly, "I'll put it in your language. Get out before I break you apart. Is that clear enough?"

The man held up a protesting hand. "Now, wait a minute."

Lebeon took him by the arm, propelling him out of the church door and down the steps. The move was none too gentle.

The man yelled back, "Trouble with you, you don't know how to sell religion."

After waiting long enough to make certain the novelty company artist had driven away, Lebeon routed Gonzalvo out to order that the mission church be locked for the first time since 1794. Then he went to his office to place a call to the bishop of the Monterey-Fresno diocese, of which Mission San Ramon was a part. He knew the bishop would be aggravated, possibly even angry. High church politics was involved in events such as "miracles."

LOCATED IN THE SMALL barrio, the Spanish-speaking neighborhood of Paso Robles, a town of about seven thousand people south of San Ramon, the two-story house was old but neat; white clapboard with frilly woodwork around the porch posts. Dr. Ramon Castillo's name was beside the door. He was a general practitioner, it said in both Spanish and English. Giron knocked, and in a moment, the porch light came on.

Dr. Castillo was young, Jose saw. Not more than thirty. He had a thick, black brush of mustache and was wearing felt bedroom slippers and a thin sweater. "What is it?" he asked in Spanish after a glance at his visitors.

"This boy needs treatment," Giron said.

"What's wrong?"

"My shoulder," Jose answered, a bit nervously.

Castillo opened the screen door and said with mild sarcasm, "Come in. I really don't have office hours. I'm just here all the time."

They followed him down the hall. What could be seen of the living room was furnished with simplicity. A young woman was in there, reading. Perhaps his wife.

The doctor turned into a door marked *"oficina,"* and they followed. He sat at his desk, pulling a pad in front of him. "Name and address."

Giron hesitated, then said, "He is not legal, doctor."

Castillo looked up. "Why did you come to me?"

"You were recommended."

Castillo said angrily, "I am sick of treating people after fights. Last week a knife wound in the abdomen, an *americano* picker. Who is doing all this recommending?"

Giron said, "The boy was not in a fight. He got a splinter in this shoulder. But he's a wetback."

Castillo shoved the pad away, cooling down, "Oh, my, the chances I take," he said. "Come on."

They went into the treatment room, and Castillo began washing his hands. "Take your shirt off. How did it happen?"

"I fell on a board."

Castillo laughed. "You're about the right age to do anything. Go sit on the stool."

The doctor pulled a light into position and felt around the shoulder. "You can't do much for a puncture but let it heal and hope nothing got inside it. I'll clean it and give you a tetanus and an antibiotic."

They were out of Castillo's office within a half hour.

Both of Jose's arms were stinging from the shots. After stopping at a hamburger stand to eat, they headed back to San Ramon in Cubria's rattling Dodge.

Midway, Jose remembered the miracle. Earlier in the evening, he'd been so worried about seeing the doctor that he'd forgotten it. "Did you hear what happened at the mission?"

Giron nodded. "It was all over the field this afternoon. But I don't believe in miracles, Jose. And I don't believe in this one, especially."

Jose was disappointed. "Why not?"

"I read the paper this afternoon. There's something strange about it. That old woman sounds crazy. The priest isn't saying much, and there was dog hair up in that loft...."

"I heard her, *señor,* when she found it."

Giron looked over. "You what?"

"I was up there."

The Dodge slowed as Giron looked over at him, mouth slightly open. "You were there?"

"Yes, *señor.*"

Giron pulled the car over and stopped, letting the engine idle. "Jose, was Sanchez with you?"

"Yes."

"And this was after you hurt your shoulder? While it was still bleeding?"

Jose nodded. "Yes."

"Oh, man. Man, oh, man. Don't you know?"

"No, *señor*."

"Put it together. That's your blood on the statue."

LATER, IN THE STORE, the tears came. He had been holding them in since Oxnard.

8

JOSEFA AND MANUEL Espinosa marched toward Mission San Ramon, Josefa straight-backed and proud; Manuel, head down, plodding sleepily beside her in the growing dawn. While it was still dark, Josefa had arisen and said her beads, then had violently shaken Manuel awake.

On reaching the front of the mission, they found Gonzalvo posted at the closed doors, a blanket draped over his shoulders against the chill. Josefa climbed the steps, half expecting Gonzalvo to bow and usher her in. But he was exhausted from all the sudden activity and only said, "Mass in the chapel! Mass in the chapel!"

"What do you mean?" Josefa asked.

Gonzalvo stared at her bleakly. She had caused all this. "Father has locked the church."

"Locked the church? How can people see Him if Father has locked the church?"

Gonzalvo said with finality, and some pleasure, "Father doesn't want anyone to see Him."

Josefa looked at the door with alarm and then glanced back at Manuel. She bounced down the steps and punched him into awareness. He fell in beside her.

All night, a sleepless night, she had been looking forward to hearing visitors say, "She saw it first, *Señora* Josefa Espinosa." She could hardly wait until mass was over to confront Father Lebeon and find out his reason for closing the church. She was so upset that she hardly participated in the mass. At its end, she waited for the priest at the chapel entrance.

"Father, why have you closed the church?"

Lebeon said quietly, "Josefa, walk with me to the sacristy."

Feeling honored by the request, Josefa said aloofly to Manuel, "Meet me in front. I must talk to Father Lebeon."

Manuel shrugged. He was only too happy to get away for a few minutes.

They walked slowly over the adobe path that led across the garden to the sacristy. Several of the white pigeons flew to the priest's shoulder, and he cooed at them, lapsing into French. Then he turned to Josefa. "I locked the church because I did not want to make a spectacle of this."

Josefa nodded gravely. That would be wrong, she knew.

"Now, if it is proved that a miracle did occur..."

"If?" Josefa wheezed, stopping abruptly. "Father, you saw it with your own eyes."

Lebeon stopped, too. "You saw a stain, and I saw one. It is still there. But we don't know what it is. You see, Josefa, if we all said it was a miracle and then it proved to be paint, how would you feel? How would we all feel? Cheated, of course."

Josefa shook her head. "It cannot be paint. It is a miracle. The wood bled. He sent us this blessing."

The priest smiled at her. "Let's wait and see."

Josefa shook her head. "You don't want a miracle."

Lebeon's face became serious, and he brushed the pigeons from his vestment. "Josefa, no one wants a miracle more than I do. It would take all day to listen to the miracles I want. Not only for you and myself and for the parish, but for all mankind. But don't you see what could happen if this is false? Some people might even lose faith."

Josefa was not listening. Her head was sagging back and forth, causing the rolls of fat beneath her chin to quiver. "You don't want a miracle."

With ringing sharpness, Lebeon said, "The church will remain closed until higher authority can determine what happened. I talked to the bishop last night, and he left it in my hands."

Josefa was stunned. She lowered herself to a bench by the garden path. "But it was there," she said. "With a shining light all around it."

Lebeon crossed the path, putting a hand on her shoulder. "I must go into the sacristy now, Josefa. All of this will be settled in time. Meanwhile, go back to your job, and I'll see you at mass in the morning."

Josefa's head went from side to side mechanically. "I quit my job yesterday so that I could be at the mission all day."

"That was a mistake," Lebeon said. "I'll call the family and see what I can do."

"I can't go back, not when there's a miracle."

Lebeon sighed. "Think about it, Josefa." He moved across the garden into the archway that led to the sacristy.

AT EIGHT O'CLOCK, Frank Olcott went to the Dinner Bell. It was a morning ritual that seldom varied. Apple juice, English muffins with honey, black coffee, and a scan of the *San Francisco Chronicle* front page.

Olcott climbed to a counter stool, was served his coffee, read the headlines, and watched the increasing flow of traffic with satisfaction. There hadn't been this many cars rolling down the Real in two years. Already, there were almost three dozen parked in front of the mission. He smiled at Maisie. "Looks like we'll have a lot of people in town today."

"Yeah, I guess so. And they'll all be coming here to the Bell 'cause they can't go over there."

"Can't go where?"

"Father locked the door last night an' ol' Gonzalvo is

guarding it like a fort. Won't let nobody in, and I mean nobody."

"I don't understand."

"Neither do I," Maisie said, "but it's a fact. Fellow came in here ten minutes ago an' said no one can get in 'til they prove it's a miracle. That's what he said."

Olcott got up and hobbled to the doorway, looking over toward the mission. Gonzalvo was there, all right. "These things sometimes take months, years."

"Maybe somebody in Santa Barbara or Fresno told him to keep people out," Maisie said. "He's got bosses. How do we know?"

Olcott said, angrily, "Well, I'm going to find out." He went back to his stool, but he'd lost his appetite and only toyed with his muffin. He went out, slamming the door.

Twenty minutes later, the cafe door opened again and Jose came in, moving timidly to a position near the front counter. *"Buenos dias,"* he said softly to the blond.

Maisie smiled at him. *"Buenos dias.* Same as yesterday?"

Jose nodded, then added, *"Un jugo."*

Maisie frowned, and a *pocho* several stools down said. "The boy wants juice."

"De naranja, por favor," Jose said.

"Orange," the *pocho* interpreted.

"Coming up," Maisie said. "Orange juice, doughnuts, *dos leche.*"

Jose nodded.

"You live near here? You're new to town."

"Si, señora."

He took the bag, paid for it, and then returned to the store. Sanchez trotted behind as he went to the front window, where he'd pulled a box up.

Giron had made him promise to tell the padre that day, but it would take a while to get the courage, and he hoped that Maldonado would arrive in time for them to go to the mission together. That priest looked as tough as the Sierra de Juárez peaks.

He'd also been thinking about the man from the service station. Surely, he knew. If Giron had been able to guess what happened, then the man, with his shining badge, had figured it out.

9

AT MID-MORNING, Olcott, flanked by Nello Solari, the big Swiss who owned the furniture store, and Abe Goldblatt, who ran San Ramon Hardware, headed toward the mission.

They passed so close to the boarded-up store that Jose pulled back from the window. He kept his eyes on Olcott as the three men crossed the street. He was certain that they were on their way to tell the padre about the false miracle. Why else would the limping man be going over there?

Then perhaps the whole town would begin searching for the person who had caused it all. Sweat popped out on Jose's forehead.

Pausing by the mission wall, Olcott counted forty people standing around. He also saw two cars pull away and move toward the freeway entrance ramp. "That's some we lost already," he said.

Josefa was sitting in the overstuffed chair, which Solari had offered the previous day. There was a small cluster of people around her. They came, listened a moment, and went on. Manuel stood behind the chair, still looking dazed.

Goldblatt said, "And that's a sight we could do without."

Solari reddened. "It's good advertising for me."

"Never mind that," Olcott snapped. "Let's go see the padre."

People had been knocking at the priest's door since the end of the second mass, and he had received each visitor with a patient explanation about the locked door. He had left his dusty rolltop desk only briefly, to accompany a laboratory technician from a Salinas hospital into the nave. The technician took a sample of the dried liquid on the statue and was now in the mission kitchen, studying the substance under a microscope. He had brought specimen slides from the hospital for comparison.

Father Lebeon had stayed with him for a few minutes but felt so uncomfortable about the use of ordinary medical techniques in such a delicate situation that he returned to his office. When he heard the rap on the door he attached a set smile to his face. He was greatly relieved when he saw who his visitors were.

"It's good to see friendly faces again. Let me get some coffee cups."

Olcott hesitated, then plunged ahead. "We didn't come to have coffee this morning, Padre."

"Well, don't tell me you're bringing a big contribution." Father Lebeon grinned over at Abe. "Know any rabbis who'd like to trade places with me today?"

Abe sputtered, the laugh sounding uneasy.

Olcott said bluntly, "Padre, we'd like to know why you closed the church."

Lebeon pushed back in his chair. "For the past two hours, I've been explaining to visitors, friends, and enemies. But you, Frank, above all, should know."

Olcott froze. "Why me?"

"Because you're a Catholic, and a very intelligent man. We can't treat this lightly; make a Las Vegas show out of it. It's got to be proved."

Recovering, Olcott said, "But people from all over the state know we've got a miracle here. It's on the radio, in the newspapers..."

"I know." Lebeon nodded. "Listen, all of you, no priest ever wanted to close a church. We'd rather open them, a thousand a day, all over the world. But something like this happens, and we can't let emotions run it. You have to be sensible. You and Nello, as parish members and citizens here, have to help me. So do you, Abe."

Olcott pulled a chair up to Lebeon's desk. He couldn't count the times he'd done this in the past two years. "Two weeks ago, Padre, I was here, in this very chair, and we talked about what could be done to save this town—put it on the map. We got no answers. But if you'll remember, when I was leaving, I said, 'Padre, maybe only luck will keep us going.' Remember that?"

Lebeon's eyes narrowed. He felt himself being trapped. "Yes, I remember."

"Well, we got that luck now. There's hope in this town again. Something's happened here. Take a walk out on the street. Go into the Dinner Bell. See for yourself. It's in the air, Padre. Don't destroy it."

"Hold on, Frank," Lebeon said angrily. "I don't want to destroy anything. I just don't want any of us to be hurt. And we can be. We can also hurt other people." The priest felt like a record on a turntable, playing the same words over and over, though to different people for different reasons. How much simpler it would be to say: Yes, it is a miracle! Hail, Mary!

Nello Solari felt compelled to speak. "We have the feeling you're against the miracle, that you won't accept it."

Lebeon looked over at Solari with puzzled anger. "Why do you have that feeling?"

Solari opened the morning Salinas newspaper and pointed to the quote from Josefa Espinosa. It said that Father Francis Lebeon, O.F.M., "had doubted her."

Lebeon said quietly, "It is my place to believe and to doubt."

Olcott's voice was just as tempered. "Padre, we're begging you to open the church. Whatever you believe about this, give your parish a chance to survive, or at least to hope. If word gets out that no one can see the statue, believe me, you personally will have finally strangled us."

Before Lebeon could answer there was a knock at the door. Lebeon called out dismally, "Come in."

It was the lab technician from Salinas. For a second, Lebeon considered asking his visitors to leave but then reconsidered. It was no time to withhold the truth. He got up from the desk and asked, "What did you find? Paint? Floor polish?"

The technician shook his head and placed two slides on Father Lebeon's desk under the lamp. "No, Father, it's blood."

Lebeon held on to the back of his chair.

"Human blood," the technician said. "Common Type O."

Lebeon felt as if he'd been slugged. Now the whole thing would mushroom. Blood didn't come out of old wood like sap. It had to be dripped on, or thrown on. Yet he still could not believe that any anyone would have the courage to do so purposely. And something else had to be considered. *Perhaps it was a miracle?*

He studied the young technician. "You're certain?"

"Positive. You can look at the slides yourself."

"Thanks very much," Lebeon said. "Will you leave these here for the commission?"

"Be glad to," the technician said.

When he had gone, Lebeon tried to muster a brave smile. "Well, it's human blood." Even he caught the hollow tone.

Abe Goldblatt, who had been silent through it all, looked at the priest with sympathy, then said, reverently, "Christ was human, Padre."

In a barely audible voice, Father Lebeon replied, "Very human, Abe." He felt tears coming into the corners of his eyes but did not know whether they were from rage or helplessness.

Olcott could not bring himself to look at the priest. The three men muttered good-bye and left without saying anything else.

Later, Lebeon set out on a stroll around San Ramon. He'd always felt these walks were as much a part of his duties as conducting mass. He was a familiar figure in the village, wearing his monk's robe in the European tradition, visiting the stores; speaking to everyone.

Jose watched him cross from the mission and again pulled back. The thought of facing him was terrifying. When the priest had disappeared up the road, he moved back closer to the grime, now imprinted here and there with the marks of his nose.

More and more people seemed to be arriving. That crazy woman never left her chair. The taco peddler was back and doing a brisk business. He'd been joined by another pushcart vendor who was selling colored ices.

Jose wondered if they were charging admission to the church.

Father Lebeon stopped first at the Dinner Bell. Maisie Keeper was polite but lukewarm. In Estaban Cole's the grocery shoppers nodded respectfully but buried themselves in their lists. Estaban didn't hide. He said, "Town's a little puzzled by what you're doin', Padre," and then decapitated a head of lettuce for emphasis.

Lebeon circled behind the stores on the west side of the Real, toward the freeway, and entered the farm-equipment shop of Freddie Lurash. Freddie turned down the spitting blue arc on his welding torch, crawled out from beneath a tractor, and lifted his goggles. He relighted the cold cigar stub in his mouth. He was a brawny little man, always greasy.

"Freddie, what's the feeling in town about my closing the church?"

Lurash sucked on his cigar a moment until the tip was red, bit a chunk off the butt, and spit it across the room. "You just walked around it, didn't you, Padre?"

Lebeon nodded. It had been an unnecessary question.

"For the first time in years they don't understand you," Lurash said. "Neither do I." Lurash had always been blunt, no matter who got offended.

"How's business?"

"Mine's great. Always is." He patted the muddy tractor. "They don't make 'em that won't break down." He peered at the priest over a cloud of thick smoke. "But some people in this town been hurtin' a long time."

Father Lebeon returned to the mission. He summoned Gonzalvo and ordered him to open the church doors. Then he sat down and carefully wrote out a request for immediate transfer from Mission San Ramon.

10

BY TWO O'CLOCK, Jose could stand it no longer. He had to see the statue. There were now more than five hundred people thronging around the mission, among them some photographers. Cars were pulling in and out every few minutes. No one would notice him, he was certain.

He crossed the Real, hearing the jingling bells from the colored-ice cart, its owner crying out, *"Helados! Helados!"* The taco man was also shouting his wares. A third peddler, holding a handful of strings attached to red and blue gas balloons, already stenciled THE MIRACLE OF SAN RAMON, was yelling, too.

It is almost like a carnival, Jose thought. *A circo.*

Then he noticed older people moving toward the church. There was a woman in a wheelchair; a man on crutches. They had to be going in for a cure. He had seen Mexicans like that going into the church in Ensenada.

How could the priest let this happen? Surely, he knew the truth. Surely, the gas station man had told him in the morning.

Jose went over near the fat woman in the chair. There was a crowd around her. He didn't understand what she was saying because she spoke in English.

"...there seemed to be a light, a beautiful light all around it..."

"And no one else was there?" a woman spectator asked.

Josefa answered regally, "It was I who discovered the Miracle of San Ramon. Father Lebeon would not believe it when I told him."

A news photographer said, "I hear he doesn't believe it now."

"He cannot doubt it."

"May I touch you?" the woman spectator asked.

Josefa considered the request and then extended her pudgy hand as if she were consecrated. "You may kiss it," she said.

The news photographer muttered, "Pardon me while I throw up," but took his photograph nonetheless.

Jose went on around the mission.

The priest was surrounded by a group of men in the garden. There were photographers and lights for television cameras. A distinguished-looking gray-haired man in a dark suit was standing near the priest.

Jose watched, certain that it concerned the statue.

"...I'm sorry about the facilities. I really wasn't expecting you in a group. I've never done anything like a press conference..."

The man in the dark suit said, "A Mr. Olcott called us last night."

Lebeon seemed puzzled.

"He said he was the mayor. I'm Jack Ortt, KDOX-TV."

Father Lebeon said, "Yes, I've seen your news shows. Well, as you see, we have..." He wondered what to say next. "Well, gentlemen, is there anything I can do for you?"

Ortt replied, "Yes, Father, the miracle."

The TV cameras began to grind as Lebeon said, "It is not really anything for sensational headlines. Or the six P.M. news, Mr. Ortt."

The newscaster replied pleasantly, "That's a matter of opinion, Father."

"It's mine. I don't choose to call this a miracle as yet." There, he thought, I've done it. The bishop would probably take exception.

"Can you explain it, then?" Ortt asked.

"I cannot," Father Lebeon replied firmly. "Look, let's not be premature. That's all I ask. These things sometimes involve hope where hope is false. Hope for old people...for the dying...for the crippled..."

Jose stood a moment longer, then forced himself to go up the church steps and inside. He stayed in the back.

Some visitors were coming in, some were leaving. A few kneeled in front of the rope. Others just stood and stared.

He looked at the stains and then at the sightless eyes angling down on him. Suddenly, he felt afraid and ran from the church. It was those eyes. He stopped a moment in the middle of the street and then kept going until he was opposite Olcott's. He hid behind a telephone pole.

Now and then, the old man's laugh drifted across the Real. He was busy. Cars were lined up at the pumps.

God will punish me; God will punish us all, Jose thought. He will cause the valley to be flooded, or open the earth.

He kept staring at Olcott and once, the old man looked up from a hood and frowned across the road.

Jose thought: You haven't told anyone. That's it. You have not told anyone. You are committing a sin as bad as mine.

11

GONZALVO SHOWED JOSE to a bench just outside the refectory, the simple dining room where the brothers ate each night. Their meal was late because there had been visitors until almost seven o'clock.

"You wait here for the padre," Gonzalvo instructed.

Jose settled down, dreading what he had to admit. Through the open refectory door he could see the brothers and the room itself. The walls were white, bare except for the wall behind Father Lebeon, who was seated at the head of the long wooden table. In a recess behind him was a crucifix.

One chair was vacant, and Jose guessed that it belonged to the monk who was by a small serving table against the wall. He was counting money. "Ninety-one, ninety-two, ninety-three . . ."

Father Lebeon suddenly barked, "Will you stop counting in here, Brother Carlos?"

The other brothers ceased eating, and there was an uneasy silence for a moment. Then Brother Carlos moved away from the side table and took his place, crossing himself, lips working in prayer.

A very young brother broke the tension. "Do you realize what all this means? Next to Lourdes and Our Lady of Guadalupe, we'll have the most famous shrine in the world."

Father Lebeon's fork stayed poised in midair. "If. If. If it's a miracle, Brother Anthony."

They all glanced at him. Then one by one they resumed eating. "You're all presupposing. We shouldn't doubt the possibility, but we should certainly question it."

Brother Carlos, who was the mission treasurer, said, "You've been negative in this from the start, Father."

"Is there something you know that we don't?" Amos asked.

Lebeon stared back at him. "I know nothing that you don't know. I'm simply more cautious. The lab tests show it was human blood. Where it came from . . . ?"

Brother Amos said, "No human would have the courage to splash blood on that statue. We agreed on that, Father."

"Most of us here were taught to believe," Brother Carlos added.

Father Lebeon rose and placed his napkin down. He said stiffly, "Excuse me," and left the refectory.

Jose started to get to his feet, but the priest swept by

without noticing him. The outside door banged shut. He stayed on the bench another moment, urging himself to follow.

Relief settled over the monks' dining room. Silverware began to clatter again.

Brother Amos said, "Aside from the other wonderful aspects of this, I'm personally not above a little larceny in my thoughts. The financial condition of this mission could use a large miracle."

"Amen," said Brother Carlos.

JOSE FOUND FATHER LEBEON standing in the garden by the mission wall, staring up the quiet road.

"Father?"

Lebeon turned and squinted into the shadows. "Yes?"

"Father, I..."

"Yes?" The priest's voice was dull and dejected.

"Is it all right if I go inside and see the statue?" He could not say anything else.

"Yes," Lebeon replied and turned away.

Jose moved quickly out of the iron gate but did not go into the church. He began to walk south, going past the Mission Bell Bar where Pook Goodwin was painting on the window. The white letters were almost complete: "Miracle Special Happy Hour—Four to Eight—Two Drinks for the Price of..."

He walked to a point opposite Olcott's, but the old man was not around. Ahead, off toward the freeway ramps, strong lights were shining, and he could see several people. He went that way.

Closer, he saw Olcott and one of the men who had gone into the mission with him in the morning. They were watching a sign painter at work under flood lights. The sign said, "See the Miracle of San Ramon." A huge arrow pointed toward the mission.

Jose went back to the store and took Sanchez out for a short walk. Returning, he sprawled down on the matting and prayed that Maldonado would arrive in the morning.

He did not sleep well.

He dreamed that he and his father were in the peaks of the Encantadas, the enchanted mountains above San Quintín. They were moving by a sheer cliff, and he fell over the side. He grabbed a root and began yelling for Maldonado to help. Jose watched as little by little the root pulled away from the side, and he plummeted down.

The last thing he saw was his father's face, looking down at him as if he'd made a mistake.

12

AN UNSEASONAL COLD front passed through the valley the next morning, bringing with it gray clouds; shrouding the Gabilans in mist. It was bleak and chilly at a few minutes after ten when an expensive maroon car with Arizona plates pulled up in front of Mission San Ramon.

A well-dressed man and his wife stepped out. The man reached back into the car and lifted out a small, thin, wheat-haired boy. He looked about five, and he was nervous, if not frightened.

Jose, seated on his box, watched from the window of the store. He had been watching since the peddlers arrived to open their pushcarts for business. The carnival had started again. At least two hundred people were already milling about.

As the man carried the boy into the church, the KDOX-TV camerman ran up, hit his switch, and aimed his lens. On the church steps, Jack Ortt said to Lebeon, "You seem to be getting more of these."

"Unfortunately," the priest replied.

"Doesn't it make you a little squeamish?"

"It does," Lebeon said flatly.

"Can't you stop it?"

Lebeon controlled his impatience. "I'm not the final authority. I have superiors who tell me a commission must decide. The town tells me the church must stay open. That's not a good answer, but that's it."

"Meanwhile," Ortt said, looking toward the door where the family had entered.

"Yes, meanwhile," Lebeon replied, and they went inside.

Lebeon watched as the couple from Arizona lighted candles. The father, holding the jittery boy erect, said, "Look, Robert. Look at the statue."

The boy gazed at it.

Lebeon fought to keep from asking the man not to do this. The child, bewildered and injured enough by whatever had crippled him, would be hurt once more.

The boy's father said, "Now, Robert, I'm going to take my hands away, and you will pray to Him that your legs will carry you. Look at the statue, think of all I've told you about it, pray very hard, and walk to the rope."

Father Lebeon listened in sick fascination, then closed his eyes to avoid seeing the rest.

He heard Ortt gasp, "He's walking! The kid's walking!"

Lebeon opened his eyes as the child took his final unsteady step toward the rope. The parents rushed forward and knelt beside him.

Instinctively, Lebeon murmured, "*Adjutorium nostrum in Nomini Domini.*" And it echoed into the far corners of his mind: "Our help is in the name of the Lord."

The priest waited until the parents and the child were leaving the church, refusing to talk to Ortt. Then he questioned the father, whose eyes were still moist. "What type of illness did the boy have?"

The man looked at Lebeon strangely. "He broke both legs two years ago. For a while, we thought there was nerve damage, but the doctor finally decided it was purely mental. Robert was afraid to use his legs."

"I see. So it wasn't physical damage."

"No."

There had been no cure, Lebeon thought. No miracle had worked. Yet, undeniably, the boy *had* walked. There was always the miracle of the human mind.

"I'd like to make a contribution," the man said.

Lebeon shook his head. "That isn't necessary. I don't think, truthfully, what happened in the church, ah... what's in the church had much to do with..." He faltered and stopped. "I, ah. Well, it's terribly difficult..."

The Arizona man interrupted softly. "Robert *is* walking."

"Yes," Lebeon agreed. "A gift will be appreciated. You can send a check."

As the car eased away, Ortt said, "Father, someone made a liar out of both of us."

"Yes, someone, or something, did." He studied the handsome, gray-haired man. "You've been a resident here for two days. You're an expert now, Mr. Ortt. How do you plan to handle this one? What will you tell your viewers? I'd be interested to know."

Ortt rubbed his jaw. "Well, the boy walked. In an odd way, your 'miracle' worked. Now, what else do I say?"

"Of all people, don't ask me." Lebeon's voice was low, defeated. He felt that he was now paying for failing to believe.

The news of the crippled boy went through San Ramon like wind-driven flames.

Jose could sense that something was different at the mission. Small groups of people were talking. The television cameramen were grinding footage of the priest as he chatted with Ortt. There were at least six people lined up to use the outdoor phone booth. Others scurried across the road.

Jose went over to the mission just before eleven. He asked the balloon peddler, who was a young *pocho*, what had happened.

"A little crippled boy found his legs in there. He walked. We have a real miracle."

"Please do not joke," Jose said. "It is a sin to joke about this."

"I'm not joking." He called over to the taco stand.

"The boy was cured," the taco cook affirmed.

Jose said, "Impossible," and began running toward the gas station.

Olcott was at the parts counter, prying into a carburetor valve with a small screwdriver when Jose entered. Olcott wasn't aware of anyone until he heard Jose saying, *"Señor, por favor, la estatua de Cristo . . . mi sangre."*

He looked up and recognized the large-eyed brown face. He dropped the valve, which hit the glass top with a cracking sound.

Jose said, *"Señor, aqui."* He pulled his shirt back to reveal the bandage. *"Mi sangre.* The mission."

Olcott's eyes narrowed.

Jose pointed to the lot next door. *"Accidente. Mi.* You help."

Olcott shook his head. "You must be crazy, boy. I've never seen you before in my life."

"Señor, por favor. Speak the padre."

Olcott was beginning to perspire. "I don't know what you're talkin' about. Get out of here."

Jose said frantically. *"Por favor, señor. Por favor."* He reached across the counter and grabbed Olcott's sleeve. "Please speak the padre."

Olcott knocked Jose's arm away and reached back of him for a tire iron. "Get out," he yelled.

Jose backed out of the service station and wheeled around toward the mission.

Olcott hobbled over to a greasy rocking chair near the oil stove and sat down heavily. His face was ashen.

JOSE WENT ALONG in an odd, disjointed half-run, half-walk. Every so often, he'd shake his head as if to dislodge something in it. Then he broke into a skip for a few yards, finally stopping about fifty feet from the church steps.

There were more visitors approaching. An elderly couple, the man leaning on a cane, were about thirty feet from the first step. A blind man was being led by his wife. A young mother and her child were almost on the top step when Jose ran for them, shouting, *"No milagro!"* He leaped and landed almost in front of them.

"No milagro," he shouted again.

The mother clutched the child to her and froze as Jose went on down the steps past them like a madman.

"Mi sangre," he yelled, separating the blind man from his wife.

The blind man flailed his arms in terror, shouting, "Helen? Helen?"

Jose grabbed him by the shoulder. *"No, señor. No milagro."*

The wife struck at him with her purse, but Jose did not feel it. He went on to the elderly couple, still yelling.

The man slashed his cane across Jose's chest, and the wife pushed him forward. He reeled against the taco cart and bounced off it. His shoulder hit the balloon peddler at the back of the knees, spilling him into the dirt.

Then Father Lebeon was pinning him down.

Almost a dozen of the red and blue balloons floated up into the sky, slowly rotating their inscriptions: THE MIRACLE OF SAN RAMON.

13

IN THE OFFICE, Father Lebeon was asking, in Spanish, "Who are you?"

Jose made his voice firm because he was no longer ashamed. "I am Maldonado's son, Jose." There was dirt on his face and a red mark on his forehead where the purse had connected. The shoulder hurt, too, where the cane had hit it. He was still breathing heavily, but he was no longer frightened. For the first time in his life, he felt confident. He knew that Maldonado would have been afraid to sit here and make the confession.

"My blood is on..."

Lebeon nodded and finished it calmly. "...is on the body of Christ."

Jose nodded.

The priest let out a long sigh, as if a weight were off him. He said "Am I glad to see you," and went back of his desk to sit down. He looked at the boy for a moment and then smiled. "Make yourself comfortable over there."

After phoning the thoroughly disgusted bishop in Fresno, telling him that he'd provide details later, Lebeon said to Amos, in English, "Get some juice for Jose, will you? Put ice cubes in it."

As Amos went out, Lebeon said, again in Spanish, "Now, tell me everything."

They were interrupted only once, when Amos returned with the glass of juice. Lebeon said, "He really deserves something much stronger, Brother Amos. I'm beginning to find out he's the only one who's been decent about this, including me."

Jose did not know what the priest was saying, but his smile was encouraging.

When he had finished telling what had happened, from his mother's death until he fell on the packing crate, Jose asked, "Will I be punished? Will you give me to Immigration?"

Lebeon was silent and thoughtful for a moment, then replied, "If anyone is to be punished, it's our mayor. For fraud, Yet he meant well, I think."

"About Immigration, Padre?"

"The first thing I think we should do is locate your father. What was the name of that company in Oxnard?"

"I think it was Consolidated. But his bosses will not let him go."

Lebeon said, "I believe they will, Jose. I'll make a

phone call, and I think they will put him in a fast car wherever he is. You see, it is illegal to hire wetbacks."

"But do not cause him trouble, please, Padre."

"I won't cause him trouble."

The priest dialed for the long distance operator and Jose listened as he began talking English to someone. Jose became anxious as Lebeon's voice rose. The priest's hard fist slammed down on the desk and his face reddened. Then he banged the phone into the cradle and leaned back in his chair.

Suddenly, he began laughing. "Your father will be on his way to Oxnard in a few minutes. I shook them up good."

Jose laughed with relief.

"Now, what are your plans?" Lebeon asked.

Jose frowned. "I have not talked about it with my father, but I want to go home."

"Back to Cabo Colnett?"

"Yes. You've never been there?"

Lebeon shook his head.

"It is far below Ensenada. Like a great bear that is always sleeping. But it is really a very friendly cape."

Lebeon smiled. "And what will you do after you get there? You said you can't live in your house any longer."

"I've been thinking about it, and I must talk to my father, but I'd like for us to build a driftwood and tin house on the beach just below Enrique . . ." He stopped.

"Go on."

"I've decided we don't need many things that people have here. Electricity is not so important. Or a motorcycle."

"Hmh," said Lebeon, thoughtfully. "And who is Enrique?"

"He is our best friend. A squatter. He fishes and catches lobster."

Lebeon said appreciatively, "You know, that sounds like a very good plan. In fact, maybe you should save a space for me. Between the bishop and the parish, I may need it."

Jose laughed softly. This priest was not so terribly tough.

Lebeon looked over at Amos, who had been quiet throughout it all. He spoke in English. "Would you call Father Glanzman? Ask him if he'll say my masses the rest of this week? I'm going to take a trip. Oxnard, and then maybe on to Ensenada."

Brother Amos appeared puzzled but finally shrugged. "Is there anything you want me to say to Frank Olcott?"

"I'll get around to Frank when I return," Lebeon replied, relishing the thought. He rose from his desk.

Jose wondered what they planned to do with him. "May I go back to the store and wait for my father?"

"I'm taking you to him. Then if I can talk him into it, I'll take both of you on to Colnett. I need to get away from here for a few days, anyhow. Otherwise, I might kick some rear ends."

A worried look passed across Jose's face. "Will there be trouble at the border, because of what we are?"

"I doubt it. My truck has Mission San Ramon painted on the side. I'll wear what I have on now. Sometimes, it's a rather handy costume. On the American side, they'll probably just smile at us and wave us through. On the Mexican side, they might even bow. A Franciscan priest with two parishioners..."

To Jose, he sounded very sure of himself. "I must get Sanchez and my suitcase. Then I'd like to say good-bye to *Señor* Giron and to thank him."

"We'll do all that." Lebeon paused briefly by the door. "Oh, Amos, you might tell the parish that my next sermon, whenever that is, is likely to have something to do with greed."

Amos nodded soberly.

There were still some people outside the mission as Jose and Father Lebeon went past the church steps. They looked at the boy and the priest and talked in low tones. The carnival was over. He'd called the bishop.

Josefa ran up. "Padre, the miracle?"

Lebeon pushed back a strong temptation to rip into her on general principles. He looked at her confused face for a moment and then smiled. "There's never been one like it, Josefa."

She beamed.

14

MALDONADO WAS SITTING on the edge of the loading dock at Consolidated, straw hat cocked back; feet dangling. He still looked like he could flick a scorpion with his fingernail.

Jose was glad to see him, but he felt strange. A lot had happened. It was not like four months ago. He'd thought about it all the way down from San Ramon.

Maldonado spotted the truck and jumped down, moving toward it with that quick, easy stride of his as Jose got out.

"Jose, Jose," he yelled, grinning widely.

"Papa."

The tall man hugged him and roughly pounded his back. "Are you all right?"

"Yes, I'm fine."

"Let me look at you." Maldonado held him off. "You are fine."

Jose nodded.

Then Maldonado saw Sanchez and frowned. "Hey, what's he doing up here?"

"He has been protecting me," Jose answered quietly.

"Protecting you?" Maldonado laughed. "No wonder there was big trouble at that farm, whatever it was." Lebeon had not gone into detail.

"Why didn't you call me at the farm, Papa?"

Maldonado frowned again. "I knew you would be all right as long as you behaved yourself. You'll have to tell me what happened."

Jose nodded.

Father Lebeon had gotten out of the truck and came over. Jose introduced him.

Maldonado took off his hat, bowed respectfully and lowered his voice. "Thank you for bringing my son, Padre. But the dog is a surprise. We did not mean to burden you with him."

"No burden," said the priest.

"We'll have to find a home for him," Maldonado said, looking over at Sanchez, tied to a rope in the back of the pickup. He was on all fours, tail wagging.

Jose stared at his father's hard, bony face. Maldonado had not changed at all. Jose loved him but did not like him. "No, Papa," he said.

Maldonado was startled.

"I'm going back to Colnett. I will take Sanchez with me."

Maldonado glanced at the priest apologetically. "He is just homesick. He has missed me. His mother died early this year."

Lebeon remained silent.

"Yes, I am homesick, Papa."

Maldonado's frown deepened. "But we must start our new life. I'll find another job and a place for us."

Jose looked at him steadily. "You can stay here, Papa. We'll see each other whenever you come to visit. I'll live with Enrique while I build my own place near his. I'll work and save money for art school. Then I'll go to Ciudad de Méjico. It will take time, I know."

"Ciudad de Méjico!" Maldonado was stunned.

Lebeon spoke up. "Why don't we get a bite to eat. Now, I don't want to interfere, but there are some things to be talked over, I imagine, as long as you two are going to separate."

Maldonado stared vacantly at the priest and then looked back at Jose, shaking his head. "Yes, Padre," he murmured.

Jose watched him as he walked back toward the loading dock to get his bag. His feet were dragging as though they were in quicksand.

AN HOUR LATER the black pickup droned south along California No. 1, the coastal freeway, at a steady fifty miles an hour. Jose sat on the old mattress Lebeon had thrown into the truck bed, suitcases near his feet. Sanchez had his head pointed into the wind. His mouth was open, and the stiff breeze pocketed in his leathers and ruffled his neck fur.

Jose turned to look through the back window. There was a trace of a smile on the priest's stubbled face, softening it. His capuche was down, forming a rich brown fold over his shoulders.

Jose stared at his father's head until Maldonado finally turned. He smiled widely and nodded; then turned to the front. It appeared that he and Father Lebeon had begun to talk again. Both men laughed as Maldonado jerked a thumb backward toward Jose and Sanchez and said something.

Perhaps there was a chance for them to understand each other now, Jose thought.

He looked down at his suitcase and was tempted to open it up and examine the paint tubes again. But the wind might blow the mounted canvasses out. He could hardly wait to get to Colnett and attempt to mix colors. If the bulldozer hadn't gone to work, the first thing he'd paint would be the old adobe. Then maybe Enrique out by his shack. In time, Maldonado out in the fields with a hoe.

Jose settled deeper into the mattress, watching the sky more than what was passing on either side. A few white fluffy clouds were adrift in it. For a short while, a hawk flew along with them and then cut a streak back toward the high brown hills.

Like the hawk, he was headed home.

About the Author

THEODORE TAYLOR

Acclaimed author Theodore Taylor was born in North Carolina and began writing at the age of thirteen, covering high school sports for a local newspaper. Before turning to writing full time, he was, among other things, a prizefighter's manager, a merchant seaman, a movie publicist, and a documentary filmmaker. The author of many books for young people, he is known for fast-paced, exciting adventure novels, including the Edgar Allan Poe award winner *The Weirdo; Air Raid—Pearl Harbor!;* and the bestseller *The Cay,* which won eight major literary awards, among them the Lewis Carroll Shelf Award. Mr. Taylor lives near the ocean in Laguna Beach, California.